Shadowlands Theatre

By

Jack J. Ward

All rights reserved.
Copyright © 2003 by Jack J. Ward
Cover art copyright © 2003 Charles Johnson

No part of this book may be reproduced or transmitted in any form or by any means, electronic or mechanical, including photographing, recording, or by any information storage and retrieval system, without permission in writing from the publisher. The characters and events in this book are fictitious. Any similarity to real persons, living or dead, is coincidental and not intended by the author.

ISBN 1-59146-008-5

crystaldreamspub.com
P.O. Box 698 Dover, TN 37058

Printed in the United States of America

CONTENTS

Acknowledgements
Forward
Preface to The Seven Deadly Sins Series
Pride: And Low Thou I Walk
Envy: Completion
Gluttony: Soul Survivor
Lust: Spin, Spin, Spin
Anger: The Hitchhiker
Greed: Ghosts of the Present

ACKNOWLEDGEMENTS

Someone once remarked to Michael Jordan that he must be lucky to be born with such a talent.
Michael reportedly shook his head and explained that the person was seeing the end product, not the hours and hours of practice time he had or the years he spent shooting hoops with his friends and family.
As human beings we do that. We focus on someone's talent as if God lowered his outstretched hand and said, "Let there be brilliance!"

But it doesn't work that way.
We are all links in an ever growing chain, with everyone we've met in our life shapes us to this moment.

I do not have time to properly name all the people who have so contributed to my growth as a writer. (Such an exercise would require a novel's length to complete!)

I will, however, name a few key players that need to take a bow with me on the stage of Shadowlands Theatre.

Andrew Dorfman. Andrew is the Yin to my Yang. Andrew is my professional and creative partner. He has drained blood, sweat, and more than a few terse choice words in creating Shadowlands. He is a singular intellect, an imaginative dynamo- director, producer, actor, and technical engineer for the creation of these plays. If just 10% of his weekly ideas are brought to fruition, the world would be a better and happier place to live.

Sylence Campbell, T.W., Keith, and all the folks at Crystal Dreams Publishing who looked at a few of my plays and said, "Yes!" Sylence is "Alexander- the Great" of this publishing effort. She has led the charge making sure this book was done on time, and done right. Her unswerving faith in my writing is legendary. My deepest thanks!

My Shadowland Theatre actors who, with their enthusiasm for this medium and my scripts, make me thrilled to sit down at my desk and pump out more. These folk fill me up when I am empty, spur dialog in the scripts, and challenge the plots without batting an eye. They give form to the characters and music to the poetry.

Christopher Moreno, who came up with the powerful theme music of Shadowlands, and sparked me to write back in high school.
To the talented singer/songwriter/musician Sharon Bee Fowler, who never hesitated to leap in to the fray and create original sound tracks and incidental music for the series.

Christy, who tasks me to be a better writer and draws me to the magic again and again;
for Deb who remains my own personal inspirational muse, well of creativity, and vibrant writing partner;
to Martin, my absent friend, never absent from my thoughts.

For my parents and my sisters who put up with the many poorly written tales of my youth.
And for my Mother especially, who edits equally wisely with broad slashes or fine surgery.
For Eddie and Sandie, my biggest fans and newest family treasure.

And for my own loving family quartet, Belinda, Aedan, Colm, and Rory, who share Husband and Father with his passion.

This book, and all others that are yet to come are dedicated to You. We sail upon the Argos together. We brave this life unto myth!

With Love,
Jack

FORWARD

In the beginning there was silence.
Writers typically begin with empty pages. Radio dramatists begin with silence. Like a singer singing a ballad, mood, setting, characters, dramatic plot, theme- an entire world- must come from sound. Not only are you tasked as writer of radio theatre to move your audience, you're required to build the pictures in their mind that tell the story.
The very first radio play "Danger" broadcast in 1924 and written by Richard Hughes understood this opportunity/ limitation from the beginning. In "Danger," Hughes' first lines of the play set the scene for everyone listening.

"What happened?"
"The lights have gone out."

From the beginning the listening audience are drawn into the coal mine and can empathize with the miners, as they feel around in the dark, looking for images and trying not to be frightened. Darkness is the tool of radio. Television has its flickering images. Cinemas are walls of exploding light. But radio capitalizes on the darkness- both within and without.

We stand together in our loneliness on radio. The heroes are without direct shape and form, so they are more easily archetypal- more easily us or someone we know. The intimacy of the audio story can reach us when we're walking with headsets, driving in our cars, sitting in a candlelit living room, , or lying in the stillness of the night in our beds. Radio edges us directly into our imagination and keys the images, sparking creativity that is as old as when we huddled together around a fire pit sharing tales of bravery, hope, and loss from storytellers.

And like storytellers, a play is not simply a tale needing to be told. It must be an experience between characters and audience. It must end well. To truly appreciate a good play, it must be meaningful. A play must be lived, not just witnessed.

Whether the conclusion of a play is happy or sad, there must be a sense of completion- a rightness that ties the play together. To leave a play and feel cheated is to know that things are left unsaid, endings are left untied. The meaning of the work is muddled and confused. Aristotle considered a good play as "catharsis" and perhaps this is what Jean-Louis Barrault meant when he wrote:

> "In fact, at the theatre, we are always assisting at a vast settlement of accounts... there should by degrees emerge a Sentence. Justice. And the spectator isn't satisfied until the sentence is just. Just, not in relation to the individuals participating in the conflict, but in relation to Life, in the universal sense of the word... Always make sure that the universal spirit of justice has been respected in a play. If not: beware of the mood of the audience."
>
> From *Reflections on the Theatre,* Jean-Louis Barrault (Rockcliff: 1951)

Meaning and the kind of justness or justice that Barrault and Aristotle depict are not necessarily some great moral authority that pronounces grand retribution or rightness upon characters. Sometimes the bad guy gets away, but at what price? Not all souls can be turned, and sometimes their wealth or failure provides a backdrop to explore our own life journey. In this, radio drama can be the most intimate connection to our inner selves. It can express the deepest pain or joy.

Begin with silence.
End with silence.
Meaning is drawn from the waking mind in its own postscript.
Just tune in.

Jack Ward, November 23rd, 2004

Preface to The Seven Deadly Sins Series

Ask any publisher and they will tell you- a series sells! If you write a group of novels based on a progressive theme like Sue Grafton's alphabetical murder mystery soup you're bound to get more sales than writing a singular novel.

So when I conceived of a series of radio plays based on the seven deadly sins, you might consider that it could potentially have continuing characters and tightly woven themes and backgrounds.

That's just not the case here. As I wrote down the seven sins, I very quickly came to the conclusion that I didn't want this to be a multi-part series with either the same hero, or the obvious theme of the sin. Each of these stories could easily stand on their own outside of the series. The stories take place in widely different backgrounds, time frames, and use different combinations of horror and suspense. Most of this comes from my abhorrence of "the formula."

Now I'm well aware, and more so each day, of the fact that good writing requires an adherence to some formulas and standards- especially when you're writing scripts. If you don't find a good rhythm in your plays you will lose your audience to another great impulse- sleep.

However, I find that even the best shows begin to tire quickly when the formula which made them great becomes so obvious that the audience comes to expect each scene before its delivered. So I decided that part of the writing of the seven deadly sins would require the audience to do a little more digging and thinking as to how the sin has affected the characters and the plot of each story. Further, I'm entranced with the idea, that each deadly sin has a virtue nestled within it.

After all, 'pride' is what can inspire us to achieve. 'Envy' can spur us onwards to improve ourselves. 'Gluttony' occurs at almost every Thanksgiving and holiday feast.

Without 'lust' most men wouldn't have gotten that part time job, or a driver's license in high school. and so on. Within each sin we have the motivating factor to become better people. It is only when the sin begins to take over our life, our common sense, and our humanity that we lose our way.

In "Ghosts of the Present" only Toby cares initially about sacking the Remus. But his greed is infectious. This occurs as well in "And Low, Thou I Walk." Here we see the fears of the church projecting a false pride within John, a certainty about his power and the righteousness of God that eventually swallows all in its path. God (or rather more precisely the vision of God in this play) is an evil force when pride is used for praise.

Of all the sins, I feel that "envy" and "sloth" are the most elusive. Thanks to J.M. Barrie, the name Wendy is now used throughout the world, but before the book "Peter Pan" it did not exist. Wendy's name becomes especially poignant in "Completion" for her flights of envy land her in a world that is ever changing and too fast for her. She feels out of place, disconnected from society. That sensation is not usually associated with envy, and yet it can be. Like sitting on the outside looking in, and pining to be part of the inner crowd, envy is a silent killer. Unlike wrath or lust, envy has little outward appearance unless you count green eyed monsters. Sloth is the same. We are a society that values free time. Those who operate slowly within this fast paced world are often hailed as "easy going" or "relaxed."
Where is the line between a peacefulness of spirit and a lack of passion? To understand which motivates someone requires a deeper look into their psyche and not just a cursory observation of their habits.

So when I began assembling these stories and attributing their motivations to the appropriate deadly sins, I recognized that the motivating factors that make us all great can easily damn us. The best of intentions really can be the road to Hell or the golden path to Heaven. The key to the destination is openness. If the protagonists in all these stories took the time to consider their actions in the greater scheme of things, and if they listened to the wisdom of those around them while filtering out the seduction of their current choices, they can be 'saved!'

In the end, there are only two real connective themes to the Seven Deadly Sins series. Each main character (even Pete Beamer) has some redeeming characteristic that makes them worthy of being saved from destruction, and that their choices to follow the allure of the sin or to be aware of the greater world around them allows an escape or condemns them to damnation.

Unfortunately for me, these are universal themes and not really standard criteria for a "series." I'd better get back to writing my great fantasy trilogies!

Note: In keeping with this theme, look for deadly sin #7 – "Sloth" – in the next collection of plays!

The Seven Deadly Sins Part #1 - Pride: And Low, Thou I Walk

And Low, Thou I Walk was first recorded at CKDU 97.5 FM in Halifax on 19th of September, 2003. The cast was as follows:

INQUISITOR	Pasha Ebrahimi
JOHN GOODMAN	Jack Ward
FRIAR	Manfred Onward
SARAH BLACK	Pamela Herman
BISHOP	Manfred Onward
CURATE	Jeff Brown
TOWNSFOLK #1,2,3,4,5	Shadowlands Theatre Players

Directors Andrew Dorfman and Jack Ward

Pride: And Low, Thou I Walk

Prologue:
There is a Land that's somewhere beyond the horizon. You may catch a glimpse of it, when the sun sets, or in the moments before dawn. It's the twilight that flickers at the edge of imagination. Somewhere between reality and fantasy. It's the place where monsters roam, and portals to other worlds wait in the back of a closet and in the crevices of your mind.
Welcome, to the Shadowlands....

Before the calling of Christ, the Sevens Sins, as much as the Seven Virtues were known in one form or another in most cultures and religions.
And yet, the first... the First sin that Lucifer committed was Pride before God.
Strange how the greatest of all sins, is considered the most potent of strengths... in the Shadowlands.

SCENE 1: Torture Room in a Small Cellar in the Church

There is a slight echo, a hollowness, when words are spoken, and the distant sounds of water droplets pooling on the floor. The surroundings are dank, dark, and unhygienic. Weak torches provide light. The inquisitor carries a torch that burns quietly but can be heard when he makes quick movements. The Inquisitor is a learned man. He wears proper clothing, and small rimmed glasses. Most times he speaks with a kind voice, rarely loudly. Dedicated to his mission, he nevertheless cares for his prisoner.
The prisoner is John Goodman. John has been tortured relentlessly and is dizzy and confused from blood loss. He is near death, and the Inquisitor needs the facts of this case before he can free John's soul to Heaven. John has passed out. The Inquisitor is beginning again.

SFX: Water droplets falling. Damp dark chamber sounds.
VFX: Slight echo when the voices grow excited.

Inquisitor: *(Gently, almost fatherly)* Please wake up...

John: mmnn...

Inquisitor: T'is time to waken... I'll let thee rest later... I promise.

SFX: Slight rattle of chains as he shifts.

John: *(Nearly cries like a waking child)...* It hurts...

Inquisitor: T'is the manacles. Don't struggle or the barbs will bleed ye more.

John: Why? Please... why?

Inquisitor: Ye know why.

John: No... I swear to Almighty God, I do not. Please. I... Who are ye...? so dark...

SFX: *Sound of a torch wavering and crackling in front of his face.*

Inquisitor: Here I am. Do ye remember me now? *(Pause)* Good... I see that ye do. What is thy name?

John: *(Crying)*

Inquisitor: This is thy last chance to see Heaven. Our Lord waits on His throne of gold. Will ye go to him?

John:*(Crying)* I want to go....

Inquisitor: *(Losing patience a little)* What is thy name?

John:*(Weakly)* John... Goodman.

Inquisitor: And why are ye here John Goodman?

John: Because... I have sinned 'gainst God... and nature.

Inquisitor: Yes. Ye have practiced the dark arts and suckle as Satan's child now. A Warlock.

SFX: *As if for the first time understanding where he is, he turns. The chains move again and he strains in pain to look*

John: The book. Where is... my book?

Inquisitor: John, the nails have cut into thy wrists again. I will wipe them. The pain helps ye to focus, but ye mustn't o'er do it. We hath thy soul to consider.

John: *(Fiercely)* The book! Where is the book!

Inquisitor: *(Taken aback but quickly falling on rhetoric)* Protect me oh Lord from yon Witches' eye. Keep me safe from his blasphemy and his dark appetite for eternal damnation. Hold me to the bosom of Our Lord's Mother, and safe within the flock as a lamb is to his shepherd.

John: *(Crying again... the sound turning to an almost frightening laughter.)*

Inquisitor: Peace John... Ye have struggled so very long now. Remember. What happened?

John: *(As if trying to remember a dream)* I... I...I... remember. Drayton.

Inquisitor: Before Drayton. Do ye remember thy mission for Christ?

John: Yes... Yes... I was on the road to Drayton Town. I was summoned. No.. sent. The Church... the church was summoned...

Inquisitor: *(More excitedly as if the story is finally coming out)* Yes, go on. Thy very soul wavers 'pon the damnable crevice.

John: There was an accusing. And the church was busy with other accusations. And...

(Defeated sounding)
...they sent me...

Inquisitor: Did ye not want to go, John?

John: No... I was happy... I wanted to rid our world of the sin that inhabits our land. The many concubines of the Beast. So much evil. They said, I was ready... I

learned as much as I could. Prepared all that I could. But nothing prepared me for what was to come...
(Sobbing softly) .. I was weak. In Jesu's name, I was so very weak...

Inquisitor: Shhh... I stand with thee now... Can ye feel this damp cloth 'pon thy head? I know t'is hard to stand, but t'will take the weight off thy manacles. Lean a little 'gainst the wall.

SFX: *Sounds of shifting chains*

(John's slight moans as he shifts position)
There... that will help thee. Now tell me John... tell me all that occurred...

John: I... I walked down the road... full of hope. I was doing God's work. I know that... even now. There was power in such clarity of being. Shining in His Grace.

Inquisitor: Tell me John.

SFX: *Torch licks out and burns John.*
VFX: *John cries out in alarm*

John... tell me. I won't let ye rest until t'is passed.

John: *(Swallows dryly)* ... Water... please? My throat is raw...

Inquisitor: Soon John. Ye weren't traveling alone?

SFX: *Distant outside sounds. Lapping lake water. Walking to the edge, then walking into the water ankle deep.*

John: ...so thirsty then too. I stopped by a river. Three weeks... No rain. T'was... part of the case... the townsfolk of Drayton had to prove her a witch. For she had fouled their crops in bitterness. I stopped by the side of the road. The path was dust, like chalk, I remember... coughing almost all day as I walked 'pon it. I bent with my face directly in the lake sucking up the water. I heard something from behind me, and in turning nearly fell in.

Friar: Good afternoon. Might I take a moment and rest here beside ye?

SCENE 2: The Friar
VFX: Voice over

John: He had a pilgrim's way of sorts. A friar I guessed by his clothes, for he wore a cloth robe, a rope belt and sandals simple in fashion. He covered his face with a hood, like the very image of mystery. He looked well-fed, even overly so. His hands were rough, with scars or boils 'pon them. His voice was quiet. It eased and unnerved me all at once. His voice wavered 'pon an accent my ears could not properly place.
I thought he'd come to be my companion... to observe how I handled the witches affair.

Friar: The water is cool?

John: Beg pardon?

Friar: Is the lake thine own, or might I drink of it?

John: Rest as thou wish, old Friar. I did not hear thy wagon.

Friar: *(Looking around him)* Janus is a quiet steed. Ye need not be alarmed.

SFX: Splashing sounds in the water

The water is not as clear as I would have it. Ye are headed West?

John: Aye, to the town of Drayton.

Friar: I hath reason to travel West as well. If ye wish to share the road a while, ye may rest thy legs 'pon my wagon.

John: Thankee, kind Friar. Have ye been traveling long?

Friar: Sometimes I feel, gentle sir... that I have been traveling since the beginning of time.

SFX: More splashing sounds in the water and drinking

The waters conceal thy reflection. I hope they do not make ye ill. I have drunk far more noxious brews in other lands and have the readier constitution. But I can tell that ye is not used to traveling, so take care... Do not develop the fever....
(A pause as John says nothing)
Ye are on God's path..?

John: It might be said, we all walk God's path.

Friar: That produces a most interesting question.

John: I had not intended it to be so.

Friar: Everything is questions gentle sir. Simple existence is a question unanswered. A quandary forever asked from mortals to God. Take Lucifer for example. He is perhaps the greatest question of all.

John: I care not to know the riddle of Satan.

SFX: They walk from the lakeside to the wagon and mount

Friar: Strange that ye use his last name, dear friend. For when he fell, he was Lucifer, but when he remained fallen, he was known as Satan... the Hebrew word not for evil, but "adversary." And no. I do not suggest that his nature after his Fall bares scrutiny.
The good book tells us what Lucifer had done, and God's punishment 'pon him for it. Much like today he was cast out. And yet once he was God's most chosen...
(Grows silent his voice thick with emotion)

John: Are ye alright Friar?

Friar: I am well, never worry, dear friend....
Lucifer was once the bringer of reason in God's court. Highest of all. None stood 'pon the right hand of God more clearly than his most treasured angel and friend. Yet, he raised armies to do battle with God. The good book speaks of what happened but it does not speak of why.

John: Pride. T'was pride that was Satan's... Lucifer's fall.. The first of all sins.

Friar: *(Sadly at John's reaction)* Aye... t'is true, and t'was right for God to cast him out, but for what reasons did Lucifer oppose his greatest benefactor, his Father, his best friend. He was given the hosts of heaven as God's fine lieutenant. Why would the greatest of God's chosen tear asunder the heavens in civil war? You speak more of who in your questioning than truly ask why?

John: What do ye mean?

Friar: I mean no insult gentle sir. But consider what ye words reveal. Ye speak of who most candidly true. For ye know the Scriptures depiction of Lucifer, and of knowing who he is through verse, we can deduce the evil and sin of his nature. On the surface, Eve's apple seemed but a rosy temptation, but there is a core to all things. Why is the most potent of all questions. When ye learn who or how, ye can gain knowledge of the events, when ye glean why, ye understand the meaning behind the events themselves. Consider Lucifer, as I have said. how could he gain followers to usurp the Kingdom of Heaven? Unless...

John: Unless...?

Friar: Unless he observed a defect within God somehow. Unless in his condemnation of God, he saw a better way - at least in his mind - to rule heaven and the Earth. For this was a time before God's loving hand shaped man. This was a time when the universe was new, and the world but a dream not yet given breath. And still, somewhere in the seven days of creation, Lucifer had seen God lacking in some way, raised an army, fought and failed.

John: Blasphemy! Ye speak blasphemy, Friar. I will not hear of such things! God is perfect. God has made all things and God alone has understanding of that which ye speak so glibly.
(Silence.)

SFX: *Only the sound of the wagon and the horse across the trail*

Friar: Forgive me, dear traveler. I meant no blasphemy, only to say that Lucifer perhaps *believed* God to be lacking... and not that he truly was. For after all, it is written - God makes no mistakes....
(Pause)
But still, I wonder to the meaning of this thing. What was it that Lucifer believed so necessary that he risked and lost all - forever cast outside of His presence.

John: Satan's fall mirrors that of man. He'd been all that we repel, and if we are worthy all that we may avoid. Satan had the choice all men have.

Friar: Indeed... I would think not.

John: He had the choice to follow God and live amongst his holy brethren in the everlasting light, or be sent to the darkness.

Friar: Aye... but ye lay thy thumb 'pon the difference 'twixt man and Satan. For which of us in experiencing God's grace and living high with Him 'pon the foot of his throne, would risk being cast from His presence?

John: None I daresay. For t'is well known that in the Light of God all sins are forgiven, and all pains are brought to an end.

Friar: But Lucifer's, my Friend. One might say, as Milton wrote, that he'd not known what he'd lost. Perhaps he felt the enterprise too great a thing, and the possibility that he would fall from His Grace unthinkable to a child born of light.

John: Perhaps... but ye speak of things that have gone far past. Satan now lives in the world. His infernal company chokes the very air of God's mercy and his hatred of our Lord knows no bounds.
(More silence)

Friar: "Had cast him out from Heaven, with all his host of rebel angels, by whose aid aspiring,
   To set himself in glory above his peers, He trusted to have equaled the Most High,
   If he opposed; and with ambitious aim, 'gainst the throne and monarchy of God....
   Him the Almighty Power, Hurled headlong flaming from th' eternal sky, With hideous ruin and combustion down,
   To bottomless perdition, there to dwell, In adamantine chains and penal fire,
   Who durst defy th' Omnipotent to arms....
   But his doom reserved him to more wrath; for now the thought both of lost happiness and lasting pain,
   Torments him; round he throws his baleful eyes, That witnessed huge affliction and dismay,
   Mixed with obdurate pride and steadfast hate...
   No light, but rather darkness visible, served only to discover sights of woe,

Regions of sorrow, doleful shades where peace and rest can never dwell, hope never comes"

SFX: *Return to the torture chamber complete with water droplets falling*
VFX: *Slight echo when the voices grow excited.*

Inquisitor: Ye speak keenly the edge of Milton, and while t'is been a source of inspiration through the clergy, I like it not. Get to the point of thy mission John. T'is my thoughts that the Friar confused ye earlier on.

John: T'was no Friar that spoke with me of that I am sure. I speak to ye now about him, for he laid the path of my misfortune and misery.

Inquisitor: Then let me wipe the blood from thy mouth, John, and pray continue. How long did ye make tracks with the Friar?

John: He spoke all through the morning with me. His thoughts about Satan's tragic loss pricked at my brain, and his questionings of God filled my head with pain. When at last he took the right fork and I the left to Drayton town, he bade me farewell and goodly profits to my enterprise. This was strange indeed, for I had not told him the reason I made for Drayton town, and yet, I could tell he scryed the reasons from me nevertheless.

SCENE 3: The Frog and the Accusation

SFX: *Sounds of the cart leaving in the distance.*
VFX: *Friar calling to the horse to continue onwards in the distance*

The final dust curtain of his cart made its unsteady way along the trail, when something caught my eye. I took several steps before I saw the body of a serpent in the road. It slithered across, perhaps intending to fang a horse, but instead was decapitated by a cartwheel and left to bleed into the soil. Its coiled form twisted and boiled in soundless anger and its severed head stared at me from the side- lipless jaws working to swallow again and again.
I would have left the ill omen there, but for the strangest sight I had yet to behold.

Inquisitor: And what was that, John?

John: From the opened end of the Serpent's gullet, something moved. I thought at first perhaps the snake was about to burst forth a series of other baby worms and held to a rock tightly to put an end to the monstrosity. But, instead there was something different.... t'was.. a frog.

Inquisitor: A frog?

John: Aye, a little tree frog. It had been swallowed whole, and even now struggled to escape from the belly of its captor. I took pity 'pon it, and with my scarf cleaned it of the snake's entrails.
It seemed quiet - or stunned.
So, I placed him in my pocket, and he became the truest of road companions.
He was quiet and slept off his excitement from before. When he awoke, he ate a little, and hopped only in a

circle about me. Then he lay down 'pon the grass to stretch his legs....

... But I did not tarry long. For I'd been charged by the Church to fulfill my service unto God. T'was just before sunset that I made the entrance to Drayton Town.

And what a sight to behold. Torchlight abounded from the village square where the townsfolk had erected a simple gallows of raised timber, nearly five feet in height so all might witness the judgment of the town.

No noose hung from the wooden post, but marks 'pon the long arm displayed that many a knot had been tied in the name of justice.

SFX: *Shouts of the villagers gathered about.*

The townsfolk gathered in a mob at sunset, and they shouted epithets and insults 'pon a woman bound to the hanging post. She was fair of skin, and young in appearance... although t'was said she was close to her thirtieth year with no husband.

Inquisitor: Yes... often such women unwilling to unify in holy wedlock, take the sheets of Satan's lustful bed.

John: She did not look afraid while they taunted her with fire and calls for her death. She bore a pride, a stubbornness, and I stepped before them in my common clothes and wide brimmed hat. So taken were they with the accusation, they'd no idea a stranger stood in their midst.

"Hold!," I said.

VFX: *Shouts of the villagers subside.*
VFX: *John's voice shouts outside.*

I am John Goodman, from Philadelphia and I have been sent by the Holy Church to measure the accused, and hear for myself the reasons the woman Sarah Black is accused of delving in the black arts....

Villager #1: She cast a drought 'pon our land! Our crops are dust and cry for water.

Villager #2: She reduced my Nancy into a cat! One day she was playing in the forest by our home, and the next she was gone with only this cat in its place. T'is witchcraft most foul! Return my Nancy! Return my Nancy to me!!

VFX: *Villagers chant together*

Mob: Return! Return! Return!

John: Hold! Hold! We live in reasoned times. And with reason we will investigate these charges. I will hear all evidence and weigh it with the Word of God... for t'is with His will that we fight the evil that would infect us.

VFX: *A whisper of ascension amidst the mob*

Mob: His will... Amen.... 'pon the cross he lay for our sins... Amen... Amen...

John: Now, one at a time, let us hear the full extent of the accusation 'pon this woman.

Villager #3: She reads her spells from the quiet of the bookstore. She sullies her father's good name by taking Satan as her bridegroom!

Villager #4: She beguiled me... and I hath neglected my husbandly duties... unable to perform as God intended man and wife to be.

Villager #5: And me as well! She brought sorrow 'pon our household and I've been unable to be with child for nigh on two years!

VFX: *John's voice over.*

John: And so it continued. Beyond the dying of the sun, and into the night. Though there were no more than a dozen accusers who'd known Sarah Black intimately, t'was becoming clear that the weight of evidence was marking hard against her soul. Slowly a picture of Sarah Black's life emerged. She's a woman who lost her father to fever some five years past and disdained all suitors, remaining wed to her grief. She began selling her father's collection of books. Well known as a God fearing man, his gentleness with his only daughter spoiled her. She withdrew from Drayton, and spurned those who proclaimed their intentions for marriage. Sarah Black lived in terrible loneliness within the bookshop.

T'was there, I had guessed that Satan's teachings transformed her. Her neighbours had always considered her willful, but now she was ne'er without a book in hand.

And t'was for her soul, in the infinite understanding of Jesus that I approached her. Her body had been given to Beelzebub... but her soul, well... I hoped a rescue from damnation was at hand.

During the hours of accusation, I'd committed each charge to memory for recounting to the Church later. I motioned for the crowd to stand back.

Reluctantly, but obediently they withdrew and I rose to the platform. The woman's hands were bound so tightly that blood trickled from the surface, and the muscles in her arms bulged bone white in effort. Although she appeared meek and mild, I'd no doubt the townsfolk bound her in such a forceful manner to ensure she could not injure herself, or others in her blasphemes.

T'was at this moment I bade her to answer the charges levied, to balance the scales to tilt her towards everlasting life rather than eternal damnation.

But of all the strange things I'd endured to this point. *(Choked emotion)* .... her words would fasten me 'pon the post beside her and set me to this damnable rack...

SCENE 4: Sarah Answers the Charges

SFX: *Return to the torture chamber complete with water droplets falling*

VFX: *Slight echo when the voices grow excited.*

Inquisitor: *(Gently almost lovingly in a whisper)* John... John... help me understand the trials ye endured. Do not risk damnation by falling silent now that the wine has been poured, and the meat is on the table. God has heard and accepted thy prayers. I've forgiven thy sins, and if thou but finish the tale, absolution awaits... I will pray with thee awhile, while our Lord and Savior collects thy soul to stand at His side and live in the immortal garden.

John: *(Dizzily... almost dream-like in his half conscious state)* Garden... yes... she smelled of flowers... gardenia... and lupins... The scent of lupins when they flower so brilliantly purple and lavender. Like the very essence of spring.

(More awake and somewhat disgusted) Most of the town smelled of raw dirt scattered about the streets, steaming from horses, and dogs, the air ripe with curing fowl, and butchered sheep. I swear in all honesty before God, I stood 'pon the gallowed deck and smelled within her the scent of Eden. I knew t'was her potions and elixirs meant for devilry and beguilement. But for a moment... a passing moment... I'd been weakened too. I felt the power of her presence.
But still... still I'd the word duty 'pon my lips and I faced her with the strength of the office 'pon my shoulders and did demand that she give full account for the accusations 'gainst her.

Inquisitor: And what did she say? This Bathsheba. This whore of Babylon?

John: T'was the strangest part of this whole venture. She neither denied nor confirmed the charges. Indeed she spoke of them not at all. Her eyes were set 'pon a distant point, and I could see she'd resigned herself to fire and death. Her face was like faded petals. She seemed not to notice me for the longest time. But I knew my purpose, and charged her again, this time *by God* , to tell me what her answer was to these charges.
She beckoned me to lean forward. I did so, though reluctantly. For while she was most handily bound to post, her eyes carried depths which frightened me.
I leaned closer, and...
(Whispering) she whispered her answer.

Inquisitor: What? What did she say?
Sarah: Teach me to heare Mermaides singing,
 Or to keep off envies stinging,
 And finde, what winde,
 Serves to advance an honest minde,
 If thou beest borne to strange sights,
 Things invisible to see,
 Ride ten thousand daies and nights,
  Till age snow white haires on thee,
 Thou, when thou retorn'est, will tell mee,
 All strange wonders that befell thee,
 And sweare, No where,
 Lives a woman, true, and faire....
(Pause)

Inquisitor: Ye are certain she spoke those words in exactly such a phrase?

John: By my troth! For once I have heard things, I cannot unhear their exact phrasing. Always I've been so gifted... since childhood.

Inquisitor: Then she spoke spells. Words of Mermaids and invisible fairies and the like. And with such words she made a confession of kinds, "No where, lives a

woman, true... and faire." She damned herself with the very spells she tried to quell thee with.
(Long pause as John considers his words.)

John: T'was Donne. I recognized it as such.

Inquisitor: And verily so! Ye saw her end, and damnable it t'was. What could ye do, but put an end to the blasphemy and pray for her soul.

SFX: The chains snap out and John snarls, startling the Inquisitor as he slips back. John sobs and falls back 'gainst the rest.

John: Its all Lucifer's fault... His sin was the first one... and it drew the line through the ages. From that one great fall, to the plagues of Egypt, the walls of Troy, the burning city of Rome about Nero... great or small we all succumb to that great fall.

Inquisitor: Pride?

John: Aye... and still we fall. Into darkness. ALL of us, Father... each in our own personal Hell.

Inquisitor: *(Growing a little tired of the indulgence)* So she was burned then John? Ye burned her.

John: Aye... But not before she cursed me!

Inquisitor: Yes... by God, ye speak more to the meat of the story. Pray take your time. How did she curse thee?

John: She whispered in my ear.

Inquisitor: She spat venom? Oft times I have heard of the evil eye and-

John: No! It t'was like rolling honey down my cheek. Sweet as summer's butter. There was no bile 'pon her words, nor bitterness within them. T'was like a gift she bestowed 'pon me. A horrid, torturous gift.

Inquisitor: What.. what did she say?

(Cries turning into maniacal laughter and back to mournful cries)
John: No! Not yet!. I cannot tell thee!

SFX: *Torturous rending 'gainst the chains.*

Inquisitor: Very well... we will return to that. Take ease, my son, and tell me all that ye are able.

John: After... after she whispered... to me... I was silent. And she would say no more. I had not wished her death. *(Roaring to the ceiling)* Sweet Grace.. please believe me!

Inquisitor: John?! John? Ye must tell what happened next?

SFX: *Distant cries of villagers, and fire, and burning planks*

John: *(Distantly)* The villagers they... they swarmed her. T'was as if they had their proof. It did not matter that I had not pronounced judgment. The faggots were struck, and the blaze burned all eyes that looked 'pon it. She was brave, and only when the apex of the pyre was lit did she cry out.

VFX: *Distant screams of Sarah burning a slight echo.*

But three times in unholy pain and regret.

SFX: *Fade townsfolk sounds back to Torture Chamber sounds.*

Inquisitor: Praise God!

John: *(Quietly disgusted)* Yes... praise God. I was shaken to the very soul. All night I spent in the quiet of the stable, hearing only the rustle of sheep. I slept not a thistle. Instead the sound of my heart pounding in immortal fear thundered in my ears, but as loud as it would roar, it could not drown her final whisper.
The next morning I resolved to leave Drayton, find the road back home, and ne'er visit this land again. The town was deserted when I left. With the menace dispatched, the men made for work in the pastures, fields and forests. No longer concerned with Sarah, they left her ash-dusted corpse on display. A warning 'gainst the evils wrought 'pon us.
I... went to her, with full desire to bury her. But...

Inquisitor: Yes? Yes? What was done? Ye should not feel such upset . T'was thy first charge, John. I keep reminding thee, but t'is true. We travel a terrible road, but it is the cross we must bear to reach His will.

John: Oh but the road, the 'terrible' road was yet to come, Father. Mayhap t'was the wind, but I swear I did not touch her person... burned clean as she was, not a streak of her lovely hair remained. I... I... stepped 'pon the ashes that ringed the grass in all directions.

SFX: *Stepping on dried out hardened grasslands. The sound of the wind lowers to almost imperceptible whispers.*

And felt the wind die in reverent protest of the will that cleansed the ground.

I would have left there with naught but the knowledge that my charge was completed. But I was entrusted with her remains.

Inquisitor: Remains?

John: All that remained of her life I found locked within her home. The townsfolk had molested the stores of books within but one remained untouched.
For fear be the greatest strength in a mob.

Inquisitor: *(Nearly babbling in haste)* Her book! A... succubus' manuscript. A tome of infernal spells!

John: ... Yes... And t'was entrusted to me to return to mother church to dispose of its sorcery. Those of Drayton wanted nothing to do with the monstrous grimoire. So emphatic their concerns that I dare not carry the book myself for fear of contamination.

Inquisitor: So afeared were ye?

John: Not at first. I was only considerate of precautions. My thoughts were to return home and to give my full accounting of what befell Sarah Black.

SFX: Wrapping the book in burlap and dragging it behind in the dirt.

So I wrapped the book several times with burlap and leather strips made of old reins from the stable, and dragged the book eight paces behind me.
My traveling companion -

Inquisitor: -The toad-

John: - Yes, the frog... had awakened amidst all the excitement and fed from my hand. He had the most soulful eyes... and

(Passing out again)

SFX: *Rattling as the chains are pulled tightly.*

Inquisitor: John keep to the story. I am not interested in your pets.

SCENE 5: The Walk Home
SFX: *Walking and nature sounds in the background*
Transitional Music

John: Yes... yes... we... we walked back from Drayton. The sky was an unnatural mottled mist that thwarted all attempts at sunlight. The sun itself appeared restrained 'gainst the southern sky. I began by and by, with each passing step, to feel a sense of forbidding dread. T'wore 'gainst my stomach. Each footfall thudded in my mind. Each yard further from Drayton increased the weight of my burden. Shadows coalesced in the trees about me. I heard the foulest whispers from the brooks I traversed. I grew aware of a presence...

Inquisitor: A presence?

SFX: *Whispers slowly growing but far in the distance.*

John: Yes... a malevolence. I could not describe it more than that. It pricked at my neck from behind and slipped from the corner of my sight and when I turned about, never to show itself directly to me. I began pausing in my gait, ostensibly to purge myself of this feeling. I began to feel alone in my quest to return to the holy church. I slept not and couldn't even light a fire, the wood would not grow hot. I shivered through the cold darkness, hearing the whispers come closer and closer until I shrieked...

VFX: *Terrified scream*

SFX: *Dead silence.*

Then silence. *(Whispering)* Not a murmur. The woods were quiet as a tomb. I lay 'gainst a tree, and swear my eyelids never crossed all the night.

SFX: *Pasture with Cattle moving*

On the second day, I had almost forgotten the night before. I was tired, but my bed would be a comfortable refuge from the hard ground, and t'was but another day hence. But I had little joy in my step. I found myself wandering through a pasture surrounded by masterless cattle that grazed without stirring. But then their heads all rose as one from the grass and their eyes bore the same red speck. I felt the wind sicken and die around me. A great unreasoning fear gripped my chest. Fire, like that which delivered the witch mirrored in their collective gaze and I began to cough from the smoke. The beasts closed around me and the whispers began again. My lungs filled with the smell of burning pitch. Everywhere I turned they faced me, tightening the circle like a noose about my neck. I wanted to drop the book, to run off. But I held tight to the strap, a mark burned across my palm and shoulder from where I held it. Then I ran. ran through the fields but the cattle followed. Lumbering they galloped as if driven off the edge of the world. The faster I ran, the more they pursued me. Finally, I tumbled down a ravine.

SFX: *Tumbling in pain down a hill.*
(Pause)

SFX: *Night sounds. Crickets and birds.*

When I awoke t'was evening. I felt a gash on my head. The moon was huge and bright as the sun and the wind had returned. My head ached where I hit the rocks below and my shoulder hurt a little, but the cattle had disappeared like a strange nightmare. I nearly laughed out loud in relief despite my circumstances, but instead I was struck dumb by the sight ahead. Within this lunar light, before me on a jagged rock the book had been torn from its bundle and lay open... naked... its pages bare before me. And...

(Choked with emotion)

Inquisitor: *(Whispering in anticipation)* and what John?

VFX: *Quiet whispering of the book growing in sound*

John: And... the pages were whispering... calling out for me to read the insidious leaves. The hoary moonlight glowed each handwritten letter. I tried to look away but I couldn't.. I just couldn't... the words. The song... t'was like... mermaids... singing to the sailors, calling them to the rocks. I crept closer... reached out -

Inquisitor: No John! In God's name, no!

John: No. No, in God's name I didn't. I cannot say by what power of grace or infamy propelled me. I cannot speak by what means, but somehow I stopped up my ears to the whispers. I bit my tongue until my eyes poured tears and the image was gone... gone.. .gone... *(Pause)*
When I awoke again the night had passed. The cool flutter of the water was like a balm to my soul. I still lay 'pon the rocks. T'was the river I had first drank from. I felt a movement in my pocket and I felt for my companion- my blessed frog. He was still a'right but seemed as dazed as I, and lay 'pon my chest lazily. T'was misty again, and near sunset by the sky so I had been sleeping through the day. My shoulder was stiff, and I felt dizzy. Frog fell asleep soon enough, and I was anxious to make my way. I replaced him in my pocket, and slowly got to my feet. I bent low to sate myself in the water, cupping my hands to wash them. When I saw her reflection.

Inquisitor: Not... the witch?!

John: No... yes... I cannot tell. For truth be told I do not know if she truly was there at all. I looked past the waters and there watching me from the other shore was a child. A waif, no more than eight or nine years, a vision, of that I was certain, a demon sent to torment me. She had the eyes of Sarah Black, soulful eyes, big and twinkling like the wings of a butterfly. I could not stand it any longer. First the cattle, and the horrible whispers, now this. I screamed at her to go away. I threw rocks to banish the apparition. But nothing would move the child-thing from its spot. I cursed it in the name of God to stop tormenting me! I swore at all the denizens in hell using every name I have ever heard a saint produce. But it would not move. I knew there was no solace for me. I had to... remove this blasphemy from my sight or I would never be free. As if in answer, the whispers began

VFX: *Quiet whispering*

again. They swallowed my mind like leeches, hungry for the blood of my sanity. I shouted and threw myself into the stream! Water foamed about me running like bile.

SFX: *Splashing*

VFX: *Gasping and heavy breathing.*

(Stone cold calm)
When the madness passed, I was drenched in the river, baptized in this unholy rite. Under my fingers I felt something limp and lifeless. I raised through the water and saw the pearl white face, the tiny body. Drowned at my hand. The eyes closed and I was safe from their burning stare. I released the body and it floated like a severed lily pad down the river and away. Free! I was finally free! The demon had tried to take me, and even in the form of a little girl, it had no power over me. No damnation could it declare, for we damn ourselves without divine intervention.
There was but only one thing left...

Inquisitor: What... what was left to do, John?

John: Why read her book of course.

Inquisitor: No! John, ye didn't.

John: I walked to the other side my clothes as heavy as my heart had been. A deathly calm 'pon me. I feared no evil, for in my pocket, my frog moved no longer.

Inquisitor: Dead like the... girl?

John: Drowned. *(Laughs hollowly)* Drowned... like my innocence.

SFX: Chain snaps out and catches the Inquisitor around the throat.

Inquisitor: *(Gasps in pain. Voice choking with the chain around it)* John... John!

John: *(Unnaturally stronger. Whispering and breathing more shallowly)* Come closer Father... for I have a story to tell and my time grows late.

Inquisitor: Jo-

John: - No... Ye wished to hear the 'poison' she whispered to me 'pon the post. And with this lash of chain about thy throat..

SFX: Tightening of the chain and a gasp from the Inquisitor

I have thy attention.

Inquisitor: *(Choking)* Enough..!

John: She said her words in sadness Father, and with no shame, but instead regret she said: .

SFX: *More struggling and chain tightening*
VFX: *Sarah's ghostly voice is heard in the background mirroring the next line*

"Read of me, and know what pregnant thoughts are lost in love."

(Pause) A curious turn of phrase for a witch to have such love is't not? I had thought it deviltry, but I learned better once I had read her journal.
T'was the church that closed her bookstore down, even the church that drove her father to his death. And the church that had taken up the struggle to protect her, though the town didn't know of it. Is't that not true, Father?

Inquisitor: *(Weakly, slowly being strangled)* John... release... release me at once... please...

John: In fact... ye were the agent of the church - one who promised to protect her... ye even gave her thine own tomes of poetry. "Teach *me* to hear Mermaides singing", Father. Ye knew she quoted John Donne, I have oft heard you say he is but your favourite poet!

Inquisitor: *(Weakly unable to call out)* Curate!

John: He cannot hear you. And any moment, the diocese will be coming. For Sarah's book lies safe within their hands.

Inquisitor: No... ye... cannot...

John: I'm certain ye will answer their questions, even their questions about indiscretions... Speak of the unborn child stilled within Sarah.
(Sarcastically) Of course it must have been her coitus with the devil!!!

SFX: *The chain is strangling the Inquisitor more and he's struggling for breath making little noise.*

Inquisitor: J- J- ggg- kkk

John: But there is still satisfaction to be had. The friar was right. The why is the question... the unanswered eternal riddle. Why... Lucifer left God... why... a Friar stepped in my path that day to warn me.. why... the death of a woman who's sin was trust and love of thee... Satisfaction must be had, dear Father. I am possessed by the devouring injustice of it... Take heart.
Thy soul will be released...
And... I... at thy hand...
Shall walk with ye...
To the banquet at the pit.
Where the answer to why... matters... not.....

SFX: *The chains and bodies go limp.*

SCENE 6: Benediction

SFX: The door is thrown back and the Curate and the Bishop descend the stairs.

Curate: But your Eminence... t'is the Holy Father's wish not to be disturbed during his interrogations.

Bishop: And how long since he's been seen from these pits?

Curate: Nearly all day, your Eminence. He's 'quired of prisoners longer in the past.

Bishop: Give me thy torch. By this night he will be placed in chains. Who was detained in this foul cellar?

Curate: An apostolate... John Goodman... I believe... *(Sees the bodies)* Saint's preserve us! Holy Father!

SFX: Tries to unwrap the chain and revive the Inquisitor.

Bishop: It matters not, Curate. They're both dead, Goodman by the bloodletting of the inquisition, and thy master by that chain about his neck.

Curate: Oh, Holy Father, what befell thee, noble man.

Bishop: Perhaps t'is best this way. He's bound by far greater laws than I now. He'll be buried outside church land-

Curate: But your Eminence surely-

Bishop: Outside! Ye heard me well enough. John Goodman, does he have family?

Curate: No... your Eminence. He was alone all his life.
Bishop: *(Pause)* Perhaps he'll find peace at last.

Epilogue:
Pride is an excessive belief in one's self. It interferes with the recognition of God's grace. Pride has been called the sin from which all other sins arise. We pride ourselves in knowing the difference between good and evil. But in our smug certainties, divine justice prevails... in the Shadowlands.

The Seven Deadly Sins Part #2- Envy: Completion

Completion was first recorded at CKDU 97.5 FM in Halifax on the 28th of May, 2003. The cast was as follows:

WENDY SMITH	Sarah Steeves
THE OPERATOR	Bob Munson
GABRIEL	Ryan Horne
ALLIE	Bea Campbell
KATE	Robin Smith
GIRL	Hazel Walling
JEFFREY	Jack Ward
TIMOTHY	Manfred Onward

Directors Jack Ward and Andrew Dorfman

Envy: Completion

Prologue:

There is a Land that's somewhere beyond the horizon. You may catch a glimpse of it, when the sun sets, or in the moments before dawn. It's the twilight that flickers at the edge of imagination. Somewhere between reality and fantasy. Its the place where monsters roam, and portals to other worlds wait in the back of a closet and in the crevices of your mind.
Welcome, to the Shadowlands....

Each day we get caught up with the little things. And yet, other people tell you its the little things in life that matter. But which little things? Are we the sum of our parts, our part of our sum? Wendy Smith is a woman in envy of the world around her. Of the stories that are occurring in other people's lives and not her own. For her part, her darkest and deepest home remains.. in the Shadowlands.

Scene 1: The Elevator

SFX: Sounds of a elevator chime and the doors closing. Wendy Smith is restless and fidgeting. She enters the elevator, turns around like always and half mumbles, half growls the first line.

Wendy: Jesus I hate this elevator.

Operator: I'm sorry.

Wendy: Every day it's the same thing. Gold lame. Gold lame. I mean.. in today's day and age, who dresses up an elevator in gold lame?

Operator: I'm sorry ma'am.

Wendy: It looks like a movie theatre you know- what? I'm sorry pardon?

Operator: I'm sorry you don't like the elevator, ma'am.

Wendy: Well, that's ridiculous. I mean, that's just ridiculous. You don't have to be sorry sir. Not one bit. I'm the one that's running off at the mouth to you every day about it... I.. I.. where was I? Oh yes, gold lame... theatre.. movies. It's dressed up like a movie theatre curtain. You know from that old theatre... that... what.. what was its name?

Operator: The Fox Theatre, ma'am?

Wendy: Yes! Yes, the Fox theatre. What a dump. Gold lame. Crinkled and pleated all the way up to the ceiling, with stains of coke, or something. Just like here. Did you ever go to that theatre?

Operator: No ma'am.. I've never been.

Wendy: Well, that's like what it is, I mean. It's like the doors would open, and I would be out on a thrust stage in front of the whole world...

Operator: I get all the theatre I need here.

Wendy: I mean, placed out for the whole world to see. I'm not ready for something like that. Who could be? *(Pause)* Wha? What? You said, you've never been? Well, let me tell you- do you have a cigarette lighter?

Operator: Me? Oh no Ma'am. I gave up smoking a long time ago.

Wendy: Yes.. I can see you're a regular boy scout. Very good. Could you do me.. um... a good turn for the day?

Operator: A deed? Certainly ma'am. *(Beat)* Where would you like to go?

Wendy: Where would I like to go? Where would I like to go? Why is it every day you ask me that question?

Operator: Beg pardon ma'am?

Wendy: The question, every day, I come in.. I complain about the gold lame walls on this shabby elevator and you ask me where I want to go. Don't you know by now?

Operator: If you would prefer not to talk on the elevator ma'am, you needn't-

Wendy: Not talk on the elevator? Why, that's a ridiculous thing to say. Ridiculous. How ever would I get to where I need to go?

Operator: Oh,... you could walk ma'am. Take the stairs. Sometimes the journey begins with a single step...

Wendy: That's good, that's good. I should get a button to stick that on for you. I like that. The journey of a single step. You forget one thing. Every morning when I come here, the elevator is right there. You're right ready to take me up. I couldn't very well turn my back on an open elevator that had lots of room, now could I?

Operator: It would seem not ma'am.

Wendy: I mean the very idea. I don't believe anyone would, you know. I mean, no matter how many times you come in sure you're going to walk those steps today. You could have set your mind to it, but before you get to the stairwell, the elevator doors open. Would you say then, "Thanks for holding the doors my good man, but I'm headed for the stairs!?"

Operator: No... I guess that wouldn't be efficient.

Wendy: Efficient be damned... it wouldn't be fast enough. We operate everything on speed. Let's say for the sake of argument- 9th floor please-

SFX: Pressing button and elevator moves
that someone would turn down a free and empty elevator, and someone with your pleasant demeanor operating it, for the staircase, you know what they would do?

Operator: I'm quite certain that-

Wendy: Exactly. Exactly! They'd run up each flight of stairs like they were riding the steeplechase to the final bend. The favoured horse to win--the elevator of course-- they imagined to be just three or four steps ahead of them. If they can only just run that much faster up the seventeen sets of stairs, then they will reach the top first, and not only would they've won the blue ribbon for health --which they wanted in the first place-- but they'd also beat the machine, and prove it was faster to take the stairs anyway. You're sure you don't have a lighter?

SFX: *There's a ding and the doors open*
Operator: Quite sure. Ninth floor ma'am. *(Beat)* Are you certain you want to get off here?

SFX: *Taken aback a bit and startled*
Wendy: Quite sure myself, thank-you.

SFX: *Exits the elevator to the busy sound of an office*
Why would you ask me if I wanted to go elsewhere?

Operator: Just curious ma'am.

SFX: *Doors closing*
Have a good day.
Wendy: *(Distantly)* Goodbye...

Scene: 2 Allie in the Office

Allie: You've got your messages on your desk, and the Simpson account is on hold on line #1. Frank wants to see you in human resources after you get settled for the day, and there's a staff lunch and learn meeting at 11:45.

Wendy: Ok... Allie?

Allie: Yes ma'am?

Wendy: How long has that elevator operator been working the elevator?

Allie: I'm sorry?

Wendy: Nothing, its ok...

SFX: *Walking to her office*
VFX: *Voice trailing off to the sounds of a busy office space*
... Which line is Fred Simpson holding on?

VFX: *Voice over*
The day flew by. I have this weird sensation on days like this. An absolute certainty that I accomplish a great many things, and do nothing at all important at the same time. I just remember a blur of contracts that were signed, seemingly endless phone calls and promises of contact lunches. By the time the day is over, I can't even remember what I'm selling- what's my part in the company, who my boss is, and why I didn't sign Allie to a lifetime contract.

Allie: You have to meet Gabe downtown.

Wendy: Gabriel? What for? Do we have a date?

Allie: *(Soft laugh)* Oh no, nothing like that... But you did promise to meet with him. Something about taking him to a family get together.

Wendy: Right... of course. Don't hover so, Allie... I think I can put on my own coat.

Allie: You'd think so. Have a good night.

Wendy: Ok.. I'll see you tomorrow. I...

Allie: What's wrong?

Wendy: I... It's nothing. I just... I think I'll take the stairs... See you tomorrow, Allie.

Allie: *(Beat)* If you think that's best.

Wendy: What?

Allie: If you get some rest...

Wendy: That's funny, I'm sure I heard you say-

Allie: Better motor... Gabe's waiting...

Scene: 3 Street and the Gabe

SFX: *The sounds of the street can be heard, cars passing, children playing. In the distance you can hear a child playing a recorder the same few notes over and over again mechanically, "hot cross buns" is the tune.*

Wendy:
VFX: *Voice over*
I walk the streets going without really knowing where- on instinct. It's like getting up in the middle of the night when you're still half-asleep and finding your way through the dark corridors to the bathroom. You know where every discarded piece of clothing fell. You know where you left the baby's rattle.

Some kids play on the street, I can't see them, but I can hear their music. A kid is trying to play "Hot Cross Buns." Every fourth line or so she gets it wrong. She always gets the fourth line wrong. Listening gives me a headache, but the more I walk it seems I can still hear the tune just off in the distance somewhere.

SFX: *The sound of an old door opening*
I find Gabriel's flat. He lives in an apartment in an old building. The art deco style is like a Gothic mansion to my modern sensibilities. It's quaint in its own way, I guess, but not my taste. Something to be said, though, for the way the architects took the time to edge in shapes and symbols along the doorway. Even the small figure of the angel crying over the old wooden double doors adds to the mood.

Gabriel meets me coming out of his apartment. It's strange. I don't know how long I've known Gabe, it seems like forever, and I've never been in his apartment. He heads me off just as I'm trying to step past him.

Gabriel: Good thing you got here. Just in time. I was about to go without you.

Wendy: Hiya Gabe. I forgot all about this party tonight. It was... um... semi-formal right?

Gabriel: *(Laughing softly)* Don't worry, you look fine. Our host won't mind at any rate.

Wendy: What's that under your arm?

Gabriel: Just my horn.

Wendy: Looks a little small for a trumpet isn't it?

Gabriel: Cornet. You never can tell when a tune is needed.

SFX: Walking. Busy Street sounds.
Wendy: I know you play in a blues band. I'm sorry Gabe.. I can't believe I've never heard you play before. You any good?

Gabriel: I play enough. I haven't played in some time though, and that's why- excuse me ma'am- that's why you haven't heard me.

Wendy: Why haven't you played? ...umm. Where are we going? I think I'm lost.

Gabriel: Pass this street, we just need to go down the 7th street fairway and then left on Elysium.

Wendy: Ok... Street's so busy it's hard to think.

Gabriel: That's the city. The right gig hasn't found me yet. Sometimes... you ever hear Count Basie play the piano?

Wendy: What does that have to do with... I mean I don't think I follow...

Gabriel: Count Basie. You know... have you heard him play?

Wendy: Well not live... if that's what you mean.

Gabriel: That's exactly what I mean. It's amazing. Sometimes he just sits there watching the band, listening and smiling, and then he'll just put out his finger and play one note on the piano... do you know what the audience does then?

Wendy: Demand their money back??

Gabriel: No, they applaud like mad. They go absolutely crazy... because Basie has captured them with one thing.

Wendy: You don't happen to have a light do you?

Gabriel: No, I don't smoke.

Wendy: *(Sighing)* I thought not...Oh well, what's that one thing?

Gabriel: He understands the power of silence. Here, just past this gate... after you..

SFX: *Sounds of a gate swinging open*
Wendy: Thanks... the power of silence?

SFX: *Walking up the cobble steps and knocking on the door gently but firmly*
Gabriel: Yes... That's the beauty of it. He waits until the perfect moment. The intervals. Basie can hear the sounds between the music. He can feel the intervals between the notes, and he understands.

Wendy: You said that... I'm glad he does... Understand?

SFX: Door opens up as Gabriel delivers the line...
Gabriel: *(Beat)* God is in the silence between the notes.

Scene: 4 The Party
SFX: *Timothy the host of the party is there. He is polite. Quiet and almost sullen.*
Timothy: Gabriel. Thanks for coming tonight. And you brought a friend.

Gabriel: Hi Timothy. This is...

Wendy: Wendy, Wendy Smith. Thanks for inviting us.

Timothy: If you'll just follow me.

Wendy: *(Whispering)* Do I know Timothy?

Gabriel: Well that depends...

SFX: *Entering a living room, soft music is being played on the piano.*
Timothy: Everyone, Gabe's brought Wendy.

SFX: *A chorus of murmured hello's and quiet welcomes*
Wendy: Well, thank you... Boy, *(laughing nervously)* this kind of reception... I feel like we've interrupted a wake....

SFX: *Dead silence. Then the sounds of furniture adjusting as if people are turning their heads.*
Gabriel: *(Leans in whispering)* Look over there Wendy... see the coffin set up against the wall?

VFX: *voice over*
Wendy: It was a wake.

SFX: *More murmurings*
Do you ever get that feeling that you're walking in a dream? Even when you're putting your foot in your mouth, it feels like you are not really there. You just retreat from the stares and the mumbles of disapproval from strangers, like you're certain that by this time next

month most of them will have forgotten what has transpired, and this time next year no one will even remember your face when you meet in someone's house with a coffin set up like a ghoulish wardrobe against a living room wall.
The evening creeps by, and I stay close to Gabe. He seems to know everyone and I know no one. That's the strange thing about a city, everyone living so close together and no one knows anyone. I suppose some feel comforted by the anonymity. They feel settled in seeing people from a distance. But for me, it just makes me nervous. I look into the faces of each of the people around me, and I know.. I mean I can feel that their lives are more full.
They have purpose. They have direction.
Every word they speak is delivered honestly. They even ask the right questions. But me, I just feel lost. I'm just walking in a dream... no worse.
Someone else's dream.

Gabriel: Did you want another piece of cake?

Wendy: Wha? I'm sorry, I must have drifted off. That couple over there. Is that the grieving family?

Gabriel: Why do you ask that?

Wendy: Because they look like they are trying to be brave about something. I've never seen people so consistently brave.

Gabriel: No. They didn't know the deceased.

Wendy: Didn't know... then why are they here?

Gabriel: You didn't know the deceased and you're here.

Wendy: I don't know why I'm here.

Gabriel: Neither do they.

Wendy: *(Someone passes Wendy cake)* Thanks...
   (Wendy thanks the server) This cake is delicious...
   (Back to Gabriel) What are their names?

Gabriel: Kate and Jeffrey. They own a boutique down in the village.

Wendy: What kind of boutique?

Gabriel: They never said.

Wendy: That sounds wonderful. They must love living down there... Just think, your own store... no... 'boutique'... in the village. Having the regulars come in and purchase the latest... the latest... well whatever the hell they sell. I bet they're happy.

Gabriel: I thought you said they looked like they were trying to be brave.

Wendy: Well, maybe I was wrong. What do I know? Look they're over by the coffin. We should go and pay our respects.

Gabriel: Wendy...

Wendy: Gabe... my arm...

Gabriel: You don't want to do that... come on its late, I should walk you home.

Wendy: Gabriel... please... its rude not to at least pay our respects, especially after everything I said earlier.

Gabriel: *(Beat)* Alright Wendy, if that's what you want.

Wendy: It will just take a moment....

SFX: *Walking sounds up to a group of people speaking)*
Jeffrey: ...- It's like one of those.. .you know.. one of those.. well.. what's that thing Katherine?

Kate: Loop.. Computer loops.

Jeffrey: Yes! That's it! Computer loops. You know, you put in the program, you punch in the numbers, but you can't get out and you need to press.. press...

Kate: Control and Break.

Jeffrey: Yes. Take control and break free.

SFX: *Murmur of ascent from the group of people, and the sound of the coffin door opening in a creak.)*
Wendy: It's empty!

Jeffrey: Why yes Wendy. Haven't you been listening to a word we've said?

Wendy: No. No. The coffin! It's empty. Where's the body?

Jeffrey: Well its not here.

Kate: Goodness no. It's long gone.

Wendy: I don't understand... then why... why...?

Jeffrey: It's better to keep that kind of unpleasantness out of sight...

Kate: Out of sight out of mind!

Jeffrey: Exactly. Exactly! Do you see that? Kate knows exactly what I mean. Three years we've been married and she nearly reads my thoughts. Wendy, are you ok? You look white as a sheet.

Wendy: I just... I guess... I guess I was expecting something different.

Jeffrey: *What* were you expecting?

Wendy: I don't know... Just... just something different... Do you have a light? I would simply just die for a cigarette...

Jeffrey: Isn't that ironic?

Allie: Are you OK, Wendy you look as white as...

Kate: A sheet...

Jeffrey: Brilliant! She never misses a mark. Do you see?

Wendy: Allie? What are you doing here? You don't happen to have a light do you?

Allie: No, sorry, I don't smoke. I'm hosting the party. I asked Gabriel to come. You look upset.

Wendy: Of course you don't smoke. I like your look, Allie. Different from what I usually see you in at the office.

Allie: What do you mean?

Wendy: I mean the nose ring and those earrings. Even the dark makeup. It looks good on you, don't get me wrong. I'm just not used to seeing you like this.

Allie: Have you been to my shop?

Wendy: Shop? You work at our office.. do.. do you have another job?

Allie: No. I don't have time. My Body Images boutique takes all my time. Do I know you from somewhere else?

Wendy: Allie... Be serious... I'm frazzled enough tonight.

Allie: I'm sorry Wendy, I don't remember meeting you before. Maybe you've got me mixed up with someone else.

VFX: Voice over
Wendy: I back away from her. She looks at me like I'm some kind of fruitcake, but I know what I know. Allie has been my office assistant for three years now. She's steady, dependable, boring. Everything you want a secretary to be. The kind of person who's idea of a night away is curling up by her radiator with a trashy romance novel, a box of Oreo cookies and a glass of milk. Someone you can call at ten o'clock at night and give instructions for the next morning. The Allie before me is an alien. Her black lipsticked mouth sneers at me. I feel stricken. I don't know what's happened. I leave as quickly as I can. I couldn't bare the humiliation of telling Gabriel about it. He never asks and I'm glad. I put him through enough tonight. The Wake. The empty coffin. The people. Allie. I was constantly on edge. I don't think I'd make it home if Gabe wasn't walking with me.

Scene: 5 Wendy's Apartment
SFX: *Sounds of going up the steps*
Well this is my stop... *(Trying to sound grateful)* Thanks for a lovely evening. I'm sorry you didn't get a chance to play your horn, Gabe.

Gabriel: There will be other times. Goodnight Wendy.

Wendy: Gabe, wait! I forgot to ask. You said, Count Basie... the silence between the music. You said something about God being in the intervals?

Gabriel: Yes.

Wendy: What did you mean about that?

Gabriel: *(Beat)* It's late. And it's not really time for the music anyway. Night Wendy.

Wendy: Gabe? Gabe! But.. but I... dammit!

VFX: *Voice over*
I feel heavy all of a sudden. Weary, like I can't take another step. Every step I take brings me closer to my bed, and I feel drawn deeper and deeper into exhaustion.

SFX: *Keys jingling*
When I fumble for my keys to get into my apartment, I feel like I've been walking for ages... lifetimes to get here. I lean against the door just to open it.

SFX: *Door opening and sound of keys jingling out of the lock. Door shuts.*
My apartment is my sanctuary, a sepulcher, and as quiet as a tomb this late at night. I just place my keys on the counter top and go to close the curtains of the front street window when I see it.

My building is the only apartment complex on the block. That's why I like it. Across from me and all around my apartment, are houses, with carefully gated, small iron fences and pristinely kept yards. Even the lampposts are those great dark green tower-like structures that are bent like... like used up dandelion flowers with their petals long gone and the seeds blown away at the end of Spring.

Hands on the curtains, ready to pull them down when something catches my eye. It's the Rezuka family, Bob and Maddie. They live right across from me. In front is their tree, the only one in a yard that's mature in the whole neighbourhood. I swear it's been here long before the pilgrims bought the island from the natives for beads. Their light's on. Not a bright one. Just the front porch light.

I know I should be in bed. I shouldn't think anything about it. I mean.. what's one light? But for some reason it just doesn't sit with me, and I pull the drapes to the window back further, the neighbours to the Rezuka's right have THEIR front porch light on. The Benjamins, and that gay couple with the schnauzer two doors beyond that, and miserable Mr. Frienklemein, the neighbourhood crank. Everyone. Everyone as far as my eye can scan past my window frame has front porch lights on.

It's a coincidence. Sure. Or it's a new policy to scare away burglars. Maybe they ALWAYS have their lights on and I just never noticed before. But.. I'm sure... I mean absolutely certain, as Christ was a Cowboy, that no one in my neighbourhood is up past eleven except me. I check the kitchen clock over the stove as it buzzes along, the second hand never stops, even for a moment in its tireless journey of time.

Midnight. 12 AM... almost on the dot. Just thirty-seven seconds until the clock strikes twelve all around the world of the city.

I'm entranced What am I waiting for? ...just midnight and people have their lights on. Why'd I trade sleep for this lunacy? Somehow I can't move from this spot- no matter how tired I am. I want to see how long this vigil of lights will continue. Will they shut off automatically on timers spent.. like fireflies, or will they stay on all night, unblinking.
I keep thinking how interesting their lives must be. Wasting such electricity- just to entertain a poor lonely, boring girl like me out from the country.
Star struck. Star struck by all the lights.
And then it happens.
If I took a long yawn, rubbed my eyes, and close them as I want to.. I'd miss it. As it was, I saw it happening. It's madness. Sheer madness. I can't understand. I just watch.

At once, like waking up on Christmas morning and stepping out of bed, they all come- out of their houses. People. Maybe a dozen people. They stretch and walk out to the street. Then they turn right as if drilling on a parade square. All in one perfect motion.
Like they share one thought, they stride down the sidewalk to the next house, then march back up the adjoined walkways. All the gates clang shut together as one...
And then without acknowledging or bowing at how masterfully its choreographed, they close the doors of their new houses, and shut off the lights.

***SFX:** sounds of distant shuffling and then closing of a dozen iron gates as one and then a dozen doors shutting as one*
I stand here. My eyes wide. Stunned. My head cranes well out beyond my window frame boundary now.

Without warning, a full 12 people that I could see clearly from my window got out of their cozy beds, walked out past their houses, stepped left and walked into new houses as if there was nothing unusual.

A moment later and all the lights in the neighbourhood wink out as one.

Scene: 6 Elevator Again
SFX: Sounds of an elevator chime and the doors closing. Wendy Smith is restless and fidgeting. She enters the elevator, turns around like always and half mumbles, half growls the first line

Wendy: Jesus, I'd kill for a smoke right now.

Operator: I'm sorry.

Wendy: I couldn't even find a match at home. I was about ready to lean over and turn up the burner on my stove, but I didn't have enough time. Do you know what I mean? You don't have a light do you?

Operator: I'm sorry, I gave up smoking-
Wendy: -A long time ago, I remember. *(Pause)* You look... tidy this morning.

Operator: I'm sorry, tidy?

Wendy: Yes... you know. Spic and span. Hospital corners clean. Sharply shaven and neatly pressed. How do you do it?

Operator: I'm sure I don't know what you mean. *(Beat)* Where to today?

Wendy: I can barely struggle out of bed, place a brush through my hair and fight into clothes and here, and you're smiling pleased as punch every morning the same. You must enjoy your job.

Operator: Its what I do. Where to?

Wendy: Where to... where to... of course where to... Ninth floor, THAT'S where to!

Operator: *(Beat)* You're sure?

(Angry pause as the elevator dings along)

Wendy: Ok... just for argument's sake, let's say that I don't want to go to the ninth floor today. Where would you recommend I go?

Operator: That's not up to me.

Wendy: Ok, let's say that it is though. Where would you in the infinite spaces between spaces within the entire seventeen floors in this office building get off at?

Operator: I wouldn't get off. It's my job to help people to their destination.

Wendy: No I mean, if you were me-

SFX: *The bell dings and the doors open. The sounds of a bustling office can be heard.*
Operator: 9th floor. *(Beat)* You sure you want to get out here?

Wendy: *(Tired sounding)* Sure... I need a smoke.

Operator: Have a good day Wendy.

(The doors close and Wendy turns around in alarm)

Wendy: How did you... I don't remember you ever...

Kate: You've got your messages on your desk, John Simpson wants you to call him back before noon. Bob has a meeting with you on your staff's performance appraisal from last week, and you've got the entire afternoon booked for the Brodicker account.

Wendy: Kate? How long have I known the elevator operator?

Kate: I'm sorry, ma'am?

Wendy: The elevator operator. Jesus, Kate he brings me up here every day, don't you take the elevator?

Kate: No I take the stairs.

Wendy: And you wouldn't happen to have a lighter?

Kate: No... sorry.

Wendy: You don't smoke. That's ok. I'm trying to quit anyway.

SFX: Walking down into Wendy's office the sounds of the busy common office area dies down
Kate: If there's nothing else? Just give me a buzz if you need me.

Scene: 7 Piercing Parlor
VFX: *Voice over*
Wendy: Ah Kate. Pure, sweet, sure as the sunrise, comforting as your favourite blankey, loyal as your childhood memories- Kate.
Sure we went through some rocky starts, three years ago. Breaking in a new assistant is always a bit of a trial, but Kate was easy. Unchanging as the sun in the sky, and as certain as night follows day.
That's the trick -- finding someone's patterns. If you can find their patterns, their habits, then all it takes is gauging what they will and won't accomplish within those parameters.
It's almost scientific, and most of us don't even spend the time watching. I'm a people person. I watch.
Most of the time though, I imagine what it would be like to be them. Ever notice that everyone around you seems to have things put together far better than you. I feel like my skin is this thin veneer. That somehow I'm just barely covering bones with my daily patterns. Some people feel trapped by their day to day grind. I think it's the only thing keeping me sane. If I didn't know precisely what was going on from moment to moment in my world, I think I'd go absolutely crackers.
Part of me wonders if that's the case for everyone. If we're all just finding one good day that worked out, and building every day around it.
Every day we try to get up the same way, just like that one good day. Brush our teeth. Go to work. Have simple meaningless conversations on the subway when necessary. Make important yet equally meaningless power meetings with people who are trying to make the same connections in work, in their personal lives, in life.

All in the name of that one good day that we can't remember, but that one good day made us think. "I want to do this forever. This is what life is about."

The day drove over me like a delivery truck making its last Friday run. I pulled myself down the stairs to the street and decided to walk a bit before heading home. I seem to remember Gabe saying something about a concert in the park. I thought maybe I could shop away the drearies on the way there.

SFX: *Street scene.. Noticeably quieter than before. Only the odd car traveling now, and people walking*
It's pretty quiet for 5:30. There's no rush hour traffic. Just a couple of cars make their way lazily down the pavement... no more than twenty or so people (by my count) out on a leisurely stroll as if they have nowhere to go, and nothing else to do but walk the streets on a weekday. Even the shops seem quiet, several of them are closed. Closed so early? Maybe I'm in an ethnic neighbourhood and there's a holiday I don't know about. It feels almost creepy, like I don't belong and I can't shake the feeling. Like the streets are pulling me.

SFX: *Strange grinding sound as the streets move to a closer perspective from Wendy. As if they were shrinking from a point around her.*
I find myself backing into a small shop, just to get away from all the openness. I didn't see what it was until I entered. The place is dark, Gothic. The smell of burning incense and gaudy crosses up on the walls with red velvet doesn't help my unease. When a young woman in her early twenties with earfuls of piercing, and lips and eyelids sparkling silver, comes over I couldn't shake the deja vu.

Allie: Can I help you Miss?

Wendy: Allie? You're Allie right?

Allie: Yeah. We met before-

Wendy: At the wake last night, I remember.

Allie: That's right. Your name is Wendy, right?

Wendy: Right... Wendy Smith. I made a big hit at the party by opening the coffin-

Allie: Right. Gutsy move...

Wendy: Yeah... What did you say his name was?

Allie: Who?

Wendy: You know, the guy in the coffin.

Allie: I didn't know him.

Wendy: You didn't?

Allie: No, my date has this thing about going to funerals... wakes even...

Wendy: *(Disappointed)* Oh, Oh I see.

Allie: Do ya want a piercing?

Wendy: Um, no. I was... ah... Just looking.

Allie: Are you sure? It'll make you a new woman.

Wendy: A new woman?

Allie: Yeah, you know, more confident.

Wendy: Really?

Allie: Yeah, and you can have it concealed. That's the great thing about most body piercings now a days. You can have them in places that aren't so noticeable, or you can be in your face with them.

Wendy: *(Not really listening)* In your face...

Allie: Sure, you know. I had this one woman in. Her husband wasn't interested any more -- at least, that was what she was complaining about. No interest in sex. You know how it is.

Wendy: Well, not really. I'm not married.

Allie: That doesn't matter. You know men. Polish their pride and joy and they'll follow you forever. So I set her up with the real thing.

Wendy: Real thing?

Allie: Tongue ring. A stud. *(Sticking her tongue out as she says it)* See?

Wendy: And that helped her? That looks painful.

Allie: No, only when it pokes through your tongue.. (*laughs suddenly*) Sorry, office humour. I mean. It helped her. Tongue studs are supposed to be excellent for fellatio.

Wendy: Is that why women get them?

Allie: *(Shrugging)* Some women sure... Me, I like the look of it.

Wendy: Doesn't it get in the way, and food?

Allie: No, I don't really notice it most of the time, and I have something else to play with when I'm bored.

Wendy: Well, thanks. I really should get going now-

Allie: You're sure I can't get you a piercing? Sometimes all you need is a change to feel like yourself.

Wendy: A change to feel like yourself. That's a little strange thinking isn't it?

Allie: *(Thinking)* I guess so... I also know it works.

Wendy: Well, maybe some other time.

Allie: You mean it?

Wendy: Well, maybe. I don't know. I've... I've got to go now. I'm late to meet someone, and I'm just dying -- you don't have a light do you?

Allie: No. Actually the incense smell comes from some filters I plug into the walls. Fire marshal rules and I don't-

Wendy: You don't smoke.

Allie: I don't smoke.

Wendy: Ok... thanks Allie. Nice to see you again.

SFX: *Stepping back to the street scene, Allie's voice comes back distant, fading*

Allie: See you... I'll be waiting.

Scene: 8 The Park

SFX: *Sounds of a car passing and then staggered walking as if Wendy is moving in a dream*
VFX: *Voice over*
Wendy: I'd be born again for a cigarette, I swear. My limbs are shaking now, as I look for home. I think I've lost my way. All the streets seem the same. Even though I only met Allie last night, It's strange, like I should know her from somewhere else. My brain is hazy like its trying to slug through mud. I'm sure my street is up here somewhere. I look left and then right. There seems to be fewer people around. Like the whole city is yawning, getting ready for bed. But it's only just after six. Why would everyone be going to sleep now?

I find the park that spans three blocks and runs adjacent to my street. It's so simple. I can't believe I missed it before. What's wrong with me? My head up in the clouds. (Pause) No one is ever going to think twice. *No one* is going to miss me if the ground just swallowed me up right now and I disappeared forever.
I feel heavy, like I can barely move again. Drunk and I haven't even had a sip. I feel like crying but I can't even manage a single tear.
I hate that. So upset that you can't even cry. So overwrought that you can't even get upset.

I can see a crowd by a bandstand. Well, maybe not much of a crowd. There may be fifteen people at the most. No one is saying anything, they are just watching. Like something caught their attention while they were walking by.
In a moment, I'm behind them. I find myself sliding between them, their bodies as still as statues. What are they watching?

VFX: *Out loud*

Excuse me... sorry... Excuse me...

VFX: *Voice over*
And then I see him. It's Gabe. And he's there standing up on the bandstand. In his hands he's holding his cornet. It looks unused, tarnished, but even in this dying sunlight it shines. It shines. He keeps putting it up to his mouth, and then back down to his chest, his head bowed. His face looks like there is something sour on the mouthpiece because he just keeps doing it over and over again. He brings the cornet up, lifts his arms and his elbows, his cheeks tighten and then just like that, he lowers the horn down to his chest, and bows his head scowling.

VFX: *Whispering to the Lady beside her*
What's he doing?

Lady in the Crowd: Don't know. He's been doing that for five minutes.

Wendy: Why doesn't he play?

Lady in the Crowd: Looks like he's having a battle with it, doesn't he?

Wendy: Why is everyone here?

Lady in the Crowd: Seemed like he's gonna play.

Wendy: No, I mean... why is everyone crowded around him right now?

Lady in the Crowd: You're here, ain't ya?

Wendy: *(Laughing softly)* You've got a good point...

Lady in the Crowd: Well, no use waiting forever is there?

Wendy: I guess not.

SFX: *Milling about. The crowd suddenly disperses on its own around Wendy*
Gabriel: I didn't see you Wendy.

Wendy: Gabe! I was hoping to hear you play.

Gabriel: I was practicing.

Wendy: Practicing? But I couldn't hear....

Gabriel: I was practicing the silence... did you like it?

Wendy: *(Laughing)* The silence! Of course, like the silences you were telling me last night. I.. I don't think the rest of the crowd appreciated your performance art.

Gabriel: I wouldn't exactly call it art. I had the mind to play maybe, but I don't think its time yet. Do you?

Wendy: I... I wouldn't know.

Gabriel: Walk you home?

Wendy: Sure. I'm just down the block here.

SFX: *Walking in silence for a bit.*
You know, Gabe, I don't know that much about you, but I can't really remember when I didn't know you.

Gabriel: Yeah? I guess I just have that kind of face... very familiar.

Wendy: What do you do?

Gabriel: Do?

Wendy: For money. I mean, since you're learning how NOT to play the horn....

Gabriel: A little of this... a little of that...

Wendy: I'm just here on the right- you don't have to tell me if you don't want to...

Gabriel: No, it's not that. "He who loses money, loses much; He, who loses a friend, loses much more; He, who loses faith, loses all."

Wendy: Oscar Wilde?

Gabriel: Eleanor Roosevelt.

Wendy: Now there was a woman.

Gabriel: Indeed.

Wendy: Can I invite you up for a coffee?

Gabriel: *(Hesitating)* No. I think I'd better be getting home. I think my dry spell may be almost over with.

Wendy: That's great news!

Gabriel: *(Beat)* For us all. Have a good night, Wendy.

VFX: *Voice over*
Wendy: I watch Gabriel leave and I can't help but get the feeling that it's the last time I'm ever going to see him. It's strange. Like when you can't take a breath, or your heart stops for a moment. You don't know if there's a moment after, when your mind screams to you and there's this horrible silence like everything is over, and its so real and unreal all in that very moment. I just watched Gabe walk away. I wanted to shout at him. I wanted to call him back up to my place. I wanted to tell

him to be safe walking home. I dunno, maybe I'm just lonely. Maybe I just want to prove I'm not alone. I don't know. Whatever it is, I just stand here, watching him walk further and further in the distance. No cars on the street now, and nobody else on the sidewalks.
And he's walking further. Walking away. Far away.

I have to tear my eyes from where he's disappeared and force myself through the door up to my apartment.

SFX: *Footsteps upstairs with a jingle of keys brought to the lock, and a door creeping open.*
My hand trembles when I find the keys to the lock. But the door opens even as I touched it.
I'm sure I locked it before I left for the office... right? Yes, of course I did.
Inside I smell the stove cooking, pots boiling. I freeze. Who's in my apartment?

I almost turned around and slinked back down the hall. Down to a neighbour to call the police. But, it's foolish. What kind of burglar makes soup in the kitchen, and leaves the lights on in the evening for everyone to see? I hold my bag tightly, and step in. Maybe it's Kate. Sure. Kate has a key. Or Mom. Yes, I sent Mom a key last Christmas and she's here. She's sorry she hasn't picked up the phone from any of my calls in the last week, and she's here making dinner for me. She knows how desperately lonely I've been, and maybe she's... I'm running now. Running through the cramped hall in my apartment to round the bend. I stop sharply at the figure in the kitchen.

VFX: *Out loud*
Who, Who are you?! What are you doing in my apartment?

Jeffrey: *(Quietly amused)* Your apartment. I pay my share too you know.

Wendy: Wha..? You're in the wrong place. Please! Please leave or I will call the cops.

Jeffrey: Dear, are you feeling all right? Look I'm sorry about last night. I shouldn't have made such a fuss. But you were ever so charming, and witty. And you always know....

Wendy: I don't know who you- wait a minute, you're, you're Jason, no... Jeff- Jeffrey... right?

Jeffrey: Really Wendy this is not a fun game. I know you've had a hellish time at work. But my day was no picnic either you know.

Wendy: But you were in the funeral party last night. With, with... Who were you with?

Jeffrey: With you Darling. We went together. Don't you remember? I mean, you walked in bold as blazes and made some kind of fuss about it being a wake. *(Still amused)* It was absolutely dazzling. They didn't know which way you were going to go next. Now sit down and let's have dinner and get you into a bath and bed...You'll feel much better in the -

Wendy: Stop! Don't! Don't move any closer! I.. I don't know who you are. I mean, I remember you from the party but that's it. Don't! I warn you. I will... I will. I'll scream if you move closer.

Jeffrey: *(Gently)* It's ok Wendy. Just relax. I'm not going to hurt you. Why would I? After all, we've been married for three years now.

Scene: 9 Girl on the Street

VFX: *Voice over*
SFX: *Panicked running down steps into the empty street*
Wendy: Running. I ran so fast out of the apartment, I nearly fell down the stairs. Jeffrey is right behind me. I swear I can feel his breath on my neck. Do you know that childhood terror? Everything is happening so fast, and you just run and run and run. And your legs go rubbery, and your chest tightens with stabbing pains and you just run and run.

It can't be more than seven o'clock at night, but everyone's gone. The city's empty as a tomb. No lights beyond the street lamps. All the buildings and houses are dark- even in the distance, like silent mountains. Shadowy distant sentinels. Watching me. I can hear only the sound of my shoes hitting the pavement. I can only feel my lungs scream as I gasp for breath. I can't .. can't get enough air. Terror freezes my chest and I feel dizzy like I'm going to tumble over and over along the concrete.

SFX: *Footfalls slowing to a staggered gate and then a kind of limping walk*
I feel the panic starting to subside. I know that either I have lost Jeffrey or he stopped trying to follow me. I'm in a back alley. It's dark. Just one street lamp making patterns like a charcoal sketch shading of a city landscape. It's all just black and white. A bleached bulb somewhere is pumping its steady antiseptic light against the dark. Like I'm looking up into a hospital lamp from a gurney. Like the last pure light anyone would see in their life.

SFX: *Sounds of walking stops and a sound of sobbing as Wendy pushes against a wall*

I'm sinking against a wall. I drop off my shoes. My feet hurt. My eyes are wet with tears. The sobs in my chest come strangled... helpless. I can't conceive of it all, of what's happening. It's all changed- changing. Am I losing my grip on sanity? Everyone else seemed happy.. at home. No one else sees the differences.
Am I losing my mind? Is it all just me? Maybe I'm the one seeing all this, and everyone else sees my husband Jeffrey.. pity's him...
Poor man, has to deal with his mad wife.
No! No. I am not married. I am alone. Alone!

One does not forget a life, just like that. One doesn't wake up one day and forget oneself, and everything they are, everything they've become. How could they do that? How could anyone do such a thing?

Girl: You ok?

VFX: *Voice over*
Wendy: I scramble back along the wall. The fear begins to overtake me again. But there's nowhere to go, I'm lost... so utterly lost.

Girl: Why are you crying?

Wendy: I'm... I'm... not... crying... I'm just... upset. Why aren't you home? Isn't it dinnertime?

Girl: I've got time. I like to play.

Wendy: I can see that... what... what are you doing?

Girl: This street has the best sidewalks. Real smooth... See... feel them. Just bend down. See... it's real smooth isn't it?

Wendy: *(Soft tension relieving laugh)* Well aren't you the brave girl. Yeah. You're right the sidewalk is smooth. Is that what you've been doing? Colouring with the chalk in your hands?

Girl: I like to draw. Do you like to draw?

Wendy: I used to... when I was a girl... just... just about your age. I used to draw comics on the street just like you. My Dad would bring home chalk... all kinds of colours, and I'd use to....

Girl: Look. I drew my Mom and my Dad here... and my sister, and my dog...

Wendy: Yes... its... just have to turn to let the light in a little. It's dark down here, but look, you've drawn the trees green, and the sky blue, and your Dad he looks strong. And your dog. That's funny, he's just like my... I forgot about that dog. I loved... I loved that dog.

Girl: Here. Wanna draw a bit? We've got time left....

Wendy: Time.... *(Another soft laugh)* ... Sure. Time... what else am I going to do...? Look. You've got three different picture squares here. You've filled the first one. I used to do that too, make the square first and then draw the picture in it. Keep inside...

Girl: Keep inside the lines! *(happily)* Just like a comic. And then you can draw a story. From beginning middle, to...

Wendy: The end. Yes yes! Ok... you finished the first one, what do you want to have for the second?

Girl: You do the last one. I'll do the next picture.

Wendy: What do you want me to draw?

Girl: What do you want to draw? You can do whatever you want. It's ok.

Wendy: (*Almost dazed*) Whatever I want... what a lovely idea. Now... now...what... what will I draw in the last picture?

Girl: Anything you want. Really, it's ok. *I'm* going to be a dancer someday. I wanna float and dance with the sugar plum fairies...

Wendy: Dancing... yes... that's a beautiful idea. Look. You've got a big space between your picture and mine... much larger than the space between your first picture and... and the one you're drawing a dancer in now.

Girl: ... you think so?

Wendy: Why yes... It's almost twice as big...

Girl: Did I do it wrong?

Wendy: Wrong? Oh no, darling, not at all. I mean, there's nothing wrong with putting more space. It gives me room. I mean, now there's more space between us while we draw. You know... it's almost... almost like...

(Pause)

Girl: hmm??

Wendy: Nothing. Just... just my friend, Gabe. He said, God is in the silence. I wonder... I wonder if he's in the gaps.

Girl: Gaps?

Wendy: Yeah, the gaps. You know between these pictures. It's so quiet in those gaps, and yet, they help you to focus. I mean, it's easy to see that you have a wonderful family and then you'll grow up to be a beautiful ballerina.

Girl: Cool!

Wendy: *(Thoughtfully)* Yeah, cool. But then... with this space, it's quiet. Don't you think? Its almost like its this long moment. This pause. Like God is trying to get our attention. Trying to tell me something. To focus on how this next picture is going to happen. What comes next? What comes next after happily ever after?

Girl: Maybe....

Wendy: Yeah, maybe?

Girl: Maybe... maybe you can draw a different picture... maybe one with a princess and dragons.

Wendy: Maybe... maybe a different story all together. I mean, if there is nothing else that can be said... then is that all there is to it?

Girl: Maybe...

Wendy: Yes? Yes?

Girl: Maybe. Maybe you could use the orange... Would that help get you started?

Wendy: *(Another soft laugh more relaxed this time)* Maybe I need some orange. What would I draw with orange?

Girl: I like to start with the sun. A good picture always starts on a new day.

Wendy: A new day... That's a good start... a sun... Something so....

Scene: 10 Beginnings
SFX: *The sound of sunrise brings a wind coming fast and furious with the heat of a new day and brightness, blinding in such a way that Wendy needs to blink before she can say the next line. The light dims again and the sounds of the elevator are humming around her.*
Wendy: Bright.

Operator: Sorry Ma'am?

Wendy: Just... just this little girl I met last night on my way home. It was really dark out, and she had the brightest chalk colours. I drew with her for a while. She had the sweetest smiles, and dreams.

Operator: Children see things differently from us. There's little that can't be accomplished when you're young.

Wendy: So many opportunities. She.. she was trying to tell me something. And it's funny. I don't think she even really knew she was telling me something. Do you know what I mean?

Operator: Where to?

Wendy: hmm? Oh... can we stop for just a moment?

SFX: *The elevator stop button is switched a soft buzz of alarm is heard for a moment but the elevator stops dead in the silence*
Operator: *(Quietly impressed)* As you wish Ma'am.

Wendy: I just... its... its just at the tip of my head. Even this morning when I woke up beside Jeffrey, I couldn't tell him. He wouldn't have understood, but... but...

Operator: You understand now?

Wendy: I think so... I think I can almost understand... I'm... I'm dead?

Operator: Oh no... Just the opposite Wendy.

Wendy: Then this isn't heaven?

Operator: Not exactly... would you like to go there?

Wendy: You mean I can?

Operator: You can choose to go wherever you want Wendy. But some choices are harder than others.

Wendy: I can still go to the ninth floor?

Operator: You can... but I don't think you want to go anymore...

Wendy: No, No... I don't. But I... I'm still afraid.

Operator: That's ok. It's ok...

Wendy: Christ you're always so easy going. Why can't you give me any answers?

Operator: I just operate the machinery. You've got to decide where you want to go. Could you do me a favour?

Wendy: Favour? You've never... I mean, sure. What is it?

Operator: Could you not call me that? I prefer my birth name.

Wendy: Call you.. wha.. Christ? I didn't mean.. I mean... I wasn't... Oh Jesus... you're...

Operator: Yes. Yes I am.

Wendy: But I meant... I wasn't calling you... I was just...

Operator: I know. But still I think a part of you knew anyway.

Wendy: I think... I think you're right. So... I'm not dead.

Operator: Just the opposite.

Wendy: I'm alive?

Operator: Not quite, but you're almost there.

Wendy: And that's where I'm supposed to go?

Operator: Right after you let all *(pause)* this... *(pause)* go.

Wendy: This?

Operator: Your life... the life you once led. The life of Wendy Smith. It's gone now. Did you have a good life?

Wendy: I... I remember now. Yes. I was married. I had a child. The girl on the street... the one who played Hot Cross Buns... the girl on the sidewalk. She was my child. She was me. She...

Operator: She reminds you of both doesn't she? She's long gone now too.

Wendy: Gone?

Operator: Just that life. She's elsewhere now.

Wendy: Elsewhere?

Operator: We all need a break sometimes. A chance to think about what our purpose is.

Wendy: But... but I thought after death we would know all.

Operator: Maybe someday... but did you ever learn anything you weren't ready to learn before?

Wendy: No... but... does (w*hispering)* does this mean there's no... God?

Operator: (*Laughing softly*) Oh no. He's there. Or She's there. Depends on how you want to look at Her or Him.

Wendy: Where?

Operator: Here... there... all around us. Just watching what we are doing. Are you ready to do it again?

Wendy: The silence... The gaps. God's in all that.

Operator: Exactly. Not in the details. He's in the quiet, in your mind. When you look out to the sea. When you listen in the forest. When you pray in Church. God's there. The details? They blind us from the whole.

Wendy: And he has a plan?

Operator: Who can say? Right now the plan is in your hands.

SFX: *The elevator switch flips and the elevator turns on again*
Where to, Ma'am?

Wendy: I think, I think I want to try another picture please. I mean... I think I'm ready to start again...

Operator: Sounds like a good choice.

SFX: The Elevator begins moving. Over the speakers plays the song "Blow Gabriel Blow"
Wendy: That... music. That's Gabe!

Operator: Yes. He can really play his horn can't he? *(Beat)* He's always been my favourite you know.

Wendy: Gabriel? I... I guess the silence has ended for him.

Operator: For all of us...

SFX: *The elevator doors open*
Just walk through the doors and all this will disappear. After all, it's just shadows of your old life. And shadows can never remain, not when there's enough sunlight.

Wendy: Oh... Jesus... its... its... a woman... and a man. She's... she's...

Operator: About to give birth. It's all there... the spark of life. A healthy young boy. Can you feel the love between them?

Wendy: It's so beautiful. The way he's holding her hand. The way she looks into his eyes. Can I go to them?

Operator: They're waiting...

Wendy: I guess... I guess. I'm finally ready. You'll tell Gabe.

Operator: He already knows.

Wendy: Will I get it right this time?

Operator: You never got it wrong last time. Remember that Ma'am. Remember it's not about that.

Wendy: I know... just... lots of colours.

Operator: Yes... (*smiling*) Use lots of colours.

Wendy: Goodbye...

SFX: Walking out into the growing light.. through the doors.
Operator: And Hello...

Epilogue:
Mrs. Wendy Smith, a woman who found out that clinging to the envy of the past keeps a soul from reaching completion, the one thing most needed in this world, the next or in- The Shadowlands.

The Seven Deadly Sins Part #3 - Gluttony: Soul Survivor

Soul Survivor was first recorded at CKDU 97.5 FM in Halifax on the 22nd of October, 2003. The cast was as follows:

LILTHRA	Laura Graham
SANDRIN	Ryan Delehanty
ELIZABETH	Elana Zatzman
MOTHER	Pamela Herman

Directors Jack Ward and Andrew Dorfman

Gluttony: Soul Survivor

Prologue:
There is a Land that's somewhere beyond the horizon. You may catch a glimpse of it, when the sun sets, or in the moments before dawn. It's the twilight that flickers at the edge of imagination. Somewhere between reality and fantasy. It's the place where monsters roam, and portals to other worlds wait in the back of a closet and in the crevices of your mind.
Welcome, to the Shadowlands....

The act of living, is the eradication of choices- narrowing down from the limitless potential of a single cell imbued with life, to the quirks and queries that make up the human experience. But how does one know which choices will ultimately be right? Or perhaps a better question to ask is, are there truly any wrong choices... in the Shadowlands.

Scene 1: In a Church

A Church organ is playing Ave Maria. Elizabeth Powers is sitting in the pew of the 7th Street Anglican Church. The collection plate is passed about. There are several dozen people sitting in the pews around her.

As the collection bowl draws near, Elizabeth is faced with a choice. Unbeknownst to her, her inner musings have set into action a timeless confrontation. With a crack of lightning both Lilthra and Sandrin appear. Lilthra is black haired and an exotic looking creature scantily dressed. Her skin is a dark ruddy colour. She displays a trace of yellow teeth and fangs. Lilthra has golden coloured eyes that are dangerous and dazzling. Adorned in what could only be considered the tightest of loincloths consisting of a smooth soundless leathery material, Lilthra's voice is rich and melodious at times, soft and almost deceptively innocent sounding at other times. She can change her demeanor at will, and is capable of appearing aggressive or submissive depending upon the situation. She is a succubus, and is an expert at using temptation to draw out sin and abandon propriety.

Sandrin is a youthful looking Angel. He is a new Deva from the Holy hosts and has yet to prove himself. He has shoulder length golden hair with eyes that appear almost similar to those of Lilthra, except they are vibrant and shining with no hint of corruption. His complexion is clear. His skin is flawless and milky white in colour. He wears a simple robe that covers his entire body, except for his hands, ankles and feet, neck, head and wings. He has a hood connected to the billowing white robe, except he has never cause to use it. His wings are magnificent, easily larger than his nearly seven foot frame, and soft as down. Lilthra is dwarfed by Sandrin's size. His expressions of piety are honest and humbling. He is innocent, but is aware of evil in the world.

Both appear sitting on the back of the pew in front of Elizabeth. They are invisible to the eyes and ears of everyone around, but are able to express their hopes and opinions to Elizabeth through her subconscious.

SFX: *A congregation in a church mulling in their chairs as the collection plate is being handed around. An organ is playing in the distance.*
   Suddenly all sounds freeze, a lightning bolt strikes. The organ holds upon a single note, and fades into the background .

Sandrin: It has happened.

Lilthra: So it has.

Sandrin: I cannot believe this. I have prepared for-

Lilthra: Elizabeth is her name.

Sandrin: I know.

Lilthra: I'm Lilthra...

Sandrin: Sandrin.. 4th fane of the 8th Precept of the 13th Rod of the Holy Hosts. I am pleased to-

Lilthra: Yes, well we'll be working together for the next..

SFX: *Sound of clipboard paper shifting*
potentially sixty-eight years on this client. Do you mind if I call you just Sandrin?

Sandrin: Not at all, Sandrin is my name.

Lilthra: Then that would certainly make it easier.

Sandrin: What would?

Lilthra:

SFX: *Scribbling on the paper*
(Mumbles to herself) No... sense.. of humour... OK...

Sandrin: What are you writing?

Lilthra: The people downstairs like to have an accurate assessment of the baseline. The good news is that after the initial paperwork on the foundations, they don't need any more written reports.

Sandrin: That is good news.. I was wonder-

Lilthra: *(Interrupting as she writes)* Be with you in a second.

SFX: *More scribbling*

Sandrin: Certainly. Take your time.

Lilthra: *(Mumbles to herself)* Takes instruction...

Sandrin: Beg pardon?

Lilthra: Please!

Sandrin: Oh.. I'm sorry..

SFX: *Furious scribbling*

Lilthra: *(Mumbles to herself)* Polite... beyond... mortal reckonin'... *(out loud)* There! That's done with then.

Sandrin: Indeed. Well then we should get going.

Lilthra: Going?

Sandrin: Yes. On this auspicious occasion of free will, the Laws of Soul Acclimatization are in effect. I, as agent of Our Father in Heaven am sent to provide guidance into the set path to righteousness and everlasting life, and you, as agent of He-Who-Has-Fallen are to provide temptation and seduction to descend from the path, into wickedness and everlasting pain...

Lilthra: Um.. Did you memorize that?

Sandrin: Beg pardon?

Lilthra: Did you memorize that? It sounds like you've memorized all 287 versus from the "Guide to Soul Protection- An Angel's Companion for the mortal world."

Sandrin: Well, yes.. You've read it?

Lilthra: Oh goodness yes.. Know thy enemy and all that stuff. Do you have the 32nd revised version?

Sandrin: 33rd actually.

Lilthra: Oh! Well then you do have a leg up on me, I'm afraid. Would you mind if I borrowed your copy for a while.

Sandrin: Sorry.

Lilthra: I thought not.

Sandrin: Do you have a manual to follow?

Lilthra: I'm afraid not. Hell isn't nearly as organized as you might think. Besides, we have this thing about infernal orders getting out. Bael is especially concerned about information leaks. He's always on about God being everywhere.

Sandrin: Well He is!

Lilthra: Then you've had to deal with it too. At any rate, you were saying...?

Sandrin: I was?

Lilthra: Yes.. about the Laws of Soul Acclimatization. In this case, Elizabeth has just turned 13, two weeks ago. Right now she's waiting for the collection plate to pass. She's reached a stage in her evolution...

Sandrin: *(Correcting)* Growth...

Lilthra: My apologies, 'growth' where she's fully cognizant of her choices. She understands the concepts of "good and evil" and in doing so is faced with her first real decision.

Sandrin: And thusly we are called.

Lilthra: Exactly... to vie for her soul until her 'natural' death- the victor to guide her to her eternal destination.

Sandrin: Heaven or Hell.

Lilthra: Not much of a choice if you ask me.

Sandrin: I am not surprised you feel that way.

Lilthra: Well, how do you want to do this?

Sandrin: According to my chit, it says that Elizabeth's mother gave her money to put in the collection plate and she's considering keeping it for video games.

Lilthra: Looks like I'm hardly needed.

Sandrin: Her thought was just a passing notion. Without your presence she would not truly be tempted.

Lilthra: So you want me here? *(Girlish twinkle)* Sandrin... you don't know how much that pleases me.

Sandrin: No.. that's not it at all. I just believe that the holy edict demands equal representation. It would do no good to simply have her go to Heaven, if there's no choice involved.

Lilthra: *(Sounding somewhat disappointed and bored)* Guess not... Well, you're new at this right?

Sandrin: What makes you think that?

Lilthra: Just call it my intuition.

Sandrin: I do not think intuition is very accurate. Relying on one's inner self as a guide removes you from Divine inspiration.

Lilthra: Well, I don't have a lot of choice in that regard, do I?

Sandrin: I would not lose faith, if I were you.

Lilthra: *(Demurely)* Why Sandrin of the 4th fane of the 8th Precept of the 13th Rod of the Holy Hosts, I do believe you're trying to save me.

Sandrin: None of us are beyond redemption Lilthra, and if I were to accept flattery for such a comment, you might consider I had pride driving it. I only wish others to return to the Light and enjoy God's grace.

Lilthra: *(Bored)* Yes.. well.. I must say, I've never been called to such a place. Imagine the first temptation here in a Church. There's a metaphor in that somehow... or an irony. I was never any good with literary terms... more interested in character development myself.

(Pause)

I'll tell you what. What if I give this one to you for free?

Sandrin: What must I do for such a bargain?

Lilthra: *(Almost under her breath)* Well at least you're willing to bargain. *(Deep breath in thought before continuing).* Nothing.. I just get the creeps in here. You've got to hand it to Christians though, while they may not have the deepest of faith in God, they certainly build structures majestic enough to cage Him.

Sandrin: I do not know where to begin with such a ridiculous statement. But I think your terms-

Lilthra: -And I get to flash the Priest.

Sandrin: Absolutely not.

Lilthra: *(Pout)* You know, I had heard the 4th fane of the 8th Precept was prudish, but I had always thought it was just one of those stories young demonesses tell damned souls to frighten them.

Sandrin: Yes, very humorous. However, you are well aware that if you reveal yourself, the client's soul is forfeited to Heaven.

Lilthra: Actually, if either of us reveals ourselves to the client, Elizabeth, then the soul is forfeited to Heaven. But trust me, the Priest is due for a thrill.

Sandrin: You would do better to focus on the soul at hand.

Lilthra: Very well.. OK.. no thrills for the clergy. If you please....?

Sandrin: Yes, of course.

VFX: *Voice echo deadens and attenuates to approximate the voice inside Elizabeth's head.*

The money is best spent in the church. It will do good works for the community, and above all make your mother proud that you are so grown up and that you know the right thing to do.

Lilthra: Very nicely put.

Sandrin: Thank-you.

Scene 2: In a Classroom
A typical grade eight class. Mostly quiet as students work furiously writing a timed test in history. Elizabeth is poorly prepared but she can clearly see the answers of Amy Murphy. She could copy those answers, as Amy is a straight "A" student and keep her high grade average. Elizabeth contemplates the severity of this choice.
SFX: *Another lightning bolt strikes and Sandrin and Lilthra find themselves sitting in a classroom.*

Lilthra: *(Holding her head)* Ohhh.

Sandrin: Are you ill?

Lilthra: I'm OK. Drinking the blood of the innocent can sometimes give you an ice-cream headache.

Sandrin: I would not know.

Lilthra: So what have you been doing since the Church?

Sandrin: That is an odd question.

Lilthra: Why?

Sandrin: Because the question is something one mortal might ask another.

Lilthra: True. Humans are strange that way. While they recognize the appearance of relativity, time is still pretty much a constant for them. It's funny when you think of it. Sure its linear like a walk to the store, but you'd think humans would learn that they don't just have to walk there, they can run, or stand absolutely still. Anyway, I was just attempting to make conversation. It's been two mortal years since I've seen you.

Sandrin: I've kept tabs on Elizabeth through that time. She's been quite faithful in her prayers.

Lilthra: Yes, ... that's just.. swell. So do you mind... ah... bringing me up to speed.. I've had a bad couple of years.

Sandrin: This is Elizabeth's eighth grade history test. She forget to study. Across from her is Amy Murphy-

Lilthra: -Right.. Riiiiiight.. it's all coming back to me. The "brain." Elizabeth can see her answers easily and if she copies she's bound to get an "A."

Sandrin: But she will have cheated.

Lilthra: Gotcha.. well it's just a little test. Certainly nothing that would put her soul in jeopardy.

VFX: *Voice echo deadens and attenuates to approximate the voice inside Elizabeth's head.*
You might make up for it later. But right now you can't afford to lose your grade point. What will Mom and Dad say?

VFX: *Sandrin's Voice echo deadens and attenuates to approximate the voice inside Elizabeth's head.*
Sandrin: You can make up for it later. You should have studied. It's something that will help you to remember in the future.

Lilthra: That's the best you've got?

Sandrin: I am just beginning. Showing her the long view is considered highly advantageous.

Lilthra: Well, if you say so. Frankly, most humans can't think in long terms. Why do you think they vote for the same party that screwed them over just two terms ago.

VFX: *Voice echo deadens and attenuates to approximate the voice inside Elizabeth's head.*

What if this is it? What if you're just not smart in History. Not as smart as you need to be. This could ruin your chances to finish the course, and then college. What will Dad say if he finds out you're lousy in his favourite subject?

VFX: *Sandrin's voice echo deadens and attenuates to approximate the voice inside Elizabeth's head.*
Sandrin: What will he say if he knows you've cheated. Elizabeth. How will he ever have faith in you again. Remember what it was like when you stole the cookie years ago. He was so disappointed. You can't disappoint him anymore Elizabeth. He believes in you. He trusts you.

VFX: *Lilthra's voice echo deadens and attenuates to approximate the voice inside Elizabeth's head.*
Lilthra: That's true. Amy's not smarter than you. She may look cuter or thinner, but she's definitely not smarter than you.

Sandrin: What are you doing?

Lilthra: Nothing...

Sandrin: You deliberately gave up.

Lilthra: I gave her something else to focus on, than to fixate on Amy's brains. Look.. I do have a reputation to protect here.. just don't make a big thing out of it, OK?

Sandrin: *(Pauses for a moment)* Are you alright?

Lilthra: I've just had a bad time of things lately.

Sandrin: I am sorry. Is there anything I can do to help?

Lilthra: You're too kind.. no really its OK. Elizabeth won't cheat this time. And I can hardly get in more trouble now anyway.

Sandrin: There's no such thing.

Lilthra: In what?

Sandrin: Being too kind. I have often wondered why humans say that, but really there is no such thing as being too kind. There is only kindness unrequited. Only then we say that someone was 'too kind.' Is that not odd to have kindness judged, not by the act itself, but rather as to how it is accepted?

Lilthra: *(In thought)* Hmm.. I've never thought of that before. You're a good Angel.

Sandrin: Thank-you.

(Pause)
So.. you are in some kind of trouble?

Lilthra: It's of no consequence to you, Sandrin. I know you're busy, and this juncture of Elizabeth's faith has passed...

Sandrin: I do not mind. If there is some way I can help.

Lilthra: Well, maybe an outsider's opinion would be good here. Even though I can probably guess what you're going to say.

Sandrin: Try me.

Lilthra: I wasn't always placed on "soul patrol" you know.

Sandrin: No. I do not know.

Lilthra: I've actually done pretty well for myself. Don't laugh.. but I've been busy (*Pause*) campaigning.

Sandrin: Campaigning? Like some large scale plot?

Lilthra: *(Laughing)* Oh Hell no! Umm.. you know. Campaigning.. politically... in Hell now for some time.

Sandrin: *(Shocked)* You have political campaigns in Hell?

Lilthra: I know.. I know.. in Heaven HE rules supreme, and its pretty much the same Below, except He likes us to organize our own governments. Its more like Mayors having to deal with a dictator. He doesn't care how the smaller governments work, in the end His edicts apply anyway.

Sandrin: So what's the point?

Lilthra: That's why I'm here. OK.. well I figured that Dis should have some sewage gutters. You know... something to funnel the blood and excrement under the city. I thought I could add something to the political debate. My slogan was, "Just because you have to live here, doesn't mean it has to be Hell."

(Silence)

Yeah... it pretty much left the arch-dark diocese speechless too. The next thing I knew, my campaign trail was over and I was sent back to the trenches.

Sandrin: That sounds pretty severe.

Lilthra: Maybe.. well, it's not important. I just.. I try to avoid most of the others when I am down here, and keep to myself. It gets lonely sometimes though.

(Pause)

Sandrin: *(Uncomfortable)*.. Well, I should get back.

Lilthra: Sure.. uh.. sorry..

Sandrin: No. No.. It is not that. I.. well, I just have to get back.

Lilthra: It's OK. *(genuine sounding)* Thanks for listening....

SFX: *Another lightning bolt strikes and Sandrin and Lilthra find themselves sitting in front seat of an idling car, the music is playing a country western tune in the background.*
Sandrin: Oh no.

Lilthra: Yes! This is the moment I've been waiting for!

Sandrin: I would not take so much pleasure in such a spectacle.

Lilthra: Nonsense! Here we are at the bluff. In a comfortable car, with a man she... well at least thinks is cute, romantic music... Our Elizabeth is about to become a woman.

Sandrin: Let us hope not!

Lilthra: You don't want her to grow up? That's sweet.. *(conspiratorially)* Come on.. I've given you the first two... now return the favour for a succubus. Let's watch!

Scene 3: In the Car
Elizabeth and Danny are in the back seat of Danny's car kissing. Sandrin and Lilthra are sitting in the front seat.

VFX: *Sandrin's voice echo deadens and attenuates to approximate the voice inside Elizabeth's head.*
Sandrin: You should wait.

VFX: *Lilthra's voice echo deadens and attenuates to approximate the voice inside Elizabeth's head.*
Lilthra: All of your friends have had sex.. you're almost 17 now. What's the big deal?

VFX: *Sandrin's voice echo deadens and attenuates to approximate the voice inside Elizabeth's head.*
Sandrin: You barely know Danny. You do not want to make love and just be used. What if he never calls you again.

VFX: *Lilthra's voice echo deadens and attenuates to approximate the voice inside Elizabeth's head.*
Lilthra: So what. So don't expect anything. You can get this out of the way.. and you'll be more experienced for someone you really love. It's a win/win. Either way, you'll still have fun. After all, you really want to. You have needs too.

VFX: *Sandrin's voice echo deadens and attenuates to approximate the voice inside Elizabeth's head.*
Sandrin: What if you get pregnant? What if he lied and he has VD or something? How could you face Mom? Dad?

Lilthra: Parental pressure. That old sausage. Sandrin... can't you come up with something better?

VFX: *Lilthra's voice echo deadens and attenuates to approximate the voice inside Elizabeth's head.*

What if he never calls you again? Maybe he'll call Amy Murphy. She probably's more fun. Skinny Amy Murphy. How can she do all those Pilates and still keep up with school? She never has trouble fitting into low cut jeans. Her Mom let *her* get her belly button pierced.

VFX: *Sandrin's voice echo deadens and attenuates to approximate the voice inside Elizabeth's head.*
Sandrin: There is no need to rush. If he is the one. You'll know. He will care about you. And if he is not, then you never did anything you would regret.

(Pause)

Lilthra: Well... damn... I guess Liz isn't going to get any after all. I hope you feel good about yourself.

Sandrin: *(Confused)* Well, of course I am pleased Elizabeth made the right choice. Her first time should be special with someone she loves.. preferably her husband.

Lilthra: Have you ever had sex?

Sandrin: I think you know the answer to that.

Lilthra: Well, then trust me.. you don't know what you're missing. The first time's always bad. Better to get it over with.

Sandrin: I don't think so. The Bible plainly states that-

Lilthra: *(Innocent joy)* -Oh.. Sandrin look.

Sandrin: Uh.. Lilthra... my hand?

Lilthra: Look!

Sandrin: Yes.. the sunset. It is lovely. But could you let go of-

Lilthra: -You know there is a secret around Hell- one that is never spoken aloud by those who visit the mortal world.

Sandrin: Is there?

Lilthra: Would you like to know what it is?

Sandrin: I am not certain.

Lilthra: Oh come on Sandrin. I promise you, you'll like it...

Sandrin: Very well.

Lilthra: *(Whispering in his ear)* Sunsets are for demons.

Sandrin: Really? Why do you believe that?

Lilthra: They are God's gift to demons. You see.. sunrises are painful. A sunrise is just too blinding for a demon to perceive, but when you see the sun set... It's like saying goodbye to the Light... and embracing the endless Night.

Sandrin: *(Genuinely impressed)* That really is... an incredible story.

Lilthra: Demons gather together to look at sunsets while on Earth... and I think most of them don't even realize why. Its true you know.
(Slight pause)
You only see the gift when it's finally leaving you.

Sandrin: Lilthra...

Lilthra: Yes Sandrin...?

(Pause)
Sandrin: Be well...

Lilthra: *(Genuine)* Thank-you Sandrin. You too.

Scene 4: Elizabeth's Bedroom.
Elizabeth is facing a vanity mirror and sitting at her desk. She stifles a sob. Elizabeth is now nearly 19 and a freshman at University taking classics. Beside her is a computer, and she turns to it and clicks on several keys.

SFX: Another lightning bolt strikes and Sandrin and Lilthra are in Elizabeth's bedroom in her dorm. Errant keyboard strokes are heard and the odd sounds of stifled tears.

Lilthra: University...

Sandrin: *(Sadly)* Yes, Elizabeth is taking the classics.

Lilthra: Don't tell me you object to Greek and Roman arts and literature too?

Sandrin: They are not my preference.. but you know that is not what troubles me.

Lilthra: What is it Sandrin?

Sandrin: I've been monitoring Elizabeth a lot lately.

Lilthra: *(Frowning)* Without me? That's not part of the contract Sandrin.

Sandrin: I have not contacted her. But I am concerned for her.

Lilthra: Personal connections are largely frowned upon by 'Him' you know.

Sandrin: Yes.. I know. *(Pause)* You were right about one thing...

Lilthra: *(Teasingly)* Sandrin! You'll make my face red!

Sandrin: Your skin is red.

Lilthra: *(Dismissive)* It's an expression.. You should work on your knowledge of the vernacular.. colours the language I think.

Sandrin: You were right about me. *(Pause)* This is my first time.

Lilthra: I thought so!

Sandrin: And because it is, I've taken some extra care. Elizabeth should not be poorly handled by any agent of God.

Lilthra: *(Dismissively)* I wouldn't worry so much if I were you. Do you actually think you're doing poorly?

Sandrin: Well.. no. I had not considered my actual performance. That would be dangerously close to pride.

Lilthra: *(Testing)* And you have no personal love for Elizabeth.

Sandrin: No.. of course not. I wish to see her reach the fields of Heaven.

Lilthra: Nothing more..?

Sandrin: Nothing more.

Lilthra: So then why so much concern. It's her choice isn't it?

Sandrin: She suffers right now.

Lilthra: *(Coldly)* Life is suffering.

Sandrin: *(Growing anger)* She suffers at your hand!

Lilthra: *(Instantly concerned sounding)* What do you mean?

Sandrin: Your words in the past few years have produced a malady within her. It eats at her spirit.

Lilthra: Sandrin... *(deep sigh)* what would you say is the watchword of Angels?

Sandrin: Watchword?

Lilthra: Watchword! A single idea formulated to produce the most effective barrier against Evil.

Sandrin: *(Pause before answering assuredly)* Vigilance. *(nods)* Certainly vigilance.

Lilthra: Thank-you for sharing that. No one would suspect the watchword of the infernal hosts.

Sandrin: Anger?

Lilthra: Nope.

Sandrin: Pride?

Lilthra: No.. *(Laughs)* although that's a great opener...

Sandrin: Envy, lust-

Lilthra: -Now you're just reciting the rest of the seven deadly sins. No, my friend. Patience... Patience! When a demon learns patience they gain nearly indomitable power. Of course, the problem is that our side of the fence wasn't born with a great deal of patience.

Sandrin: Certainly not. He-Who-Is-Cast-Out is an example of that.

Lilthra: Well, I will not speak ill of my Father Below, however... he *has* learned patience, of late. His anger is ever growing. His impatience may be waxing, but he's still *practicing* patience. Why do you think the lost souls are tortured so?

Sandrin: Punishment.

Lilthra: For what? We won them... fair and square... sometimes by hook or by crook. There's no need to punish those who have fallen in with us. We're at war, but the war is over for them. No.. they are tormented and brutally so.. A distraction for His impatience.

Sandrin: How horrible!

Lilthra: But not inconceivable. A father comes home and spanks his child for a wayward look. It's therapy... releases the anger he holds for his boss.

Sandrin: That's monstrous!

Lilthra: *(Sympathetically)* Oh, I know. And you know as much as I'd encourage such exorcising of demons in my job, *(smiling)* I certainly wouldn't enjoy it.

Sandrin: If that's true.. then why spread poison in Elizabeth?

Lilthra: *(Straight)* You're not listening, Sandrin. It's my job.

Sandrin: *(Coldly)* Your job is to tempt, not illicit malefic ideas that never originated from Elizabeth.

Lilthra: *(Patiently, almost paternally)* The "client" Sandrin. Remember, she's just assigned to us.

Sandrin: Do not avoid the question.

Lilthra: *(Playful avoidance)* Look.. she's going through her e-mail. Isn't that a pain in the ass? I mean, the junk mail that gets sent to people. How could someone possibly want a penis enlargement and a breast enlargement at the same time? Come on people! *(Claps hands to get attention)* Get your spam working together! Does *everyone's* market research assume we're all she-males...?!

Sandrin: Lilthra...

Lilthra: ...SOMEONE should lose their job for that!!!

Sandrin: Lilthra!

Lilthra: *(Pause and then more seriously)* Alright.. patience. Like I was saying. Evil is not one left turn on the glittering highway. It's not one minute you wake up and you've been transformed into a selfish person... life just beats it into you. Human beings are so incapable of looking at the larger scheme of things, and so utterly devoured with their sense of self.

Sandrin: Why di-

Lilthra: Gluttony. Sure it made the top seven list, but its *SO* very understated if you ask me. Angels are very aware of Pride. They don't call it the 'Big One' for nothing, and lust is a commodity as easy to sell as envy. But gluttony? Gluttony takes a *special* kind of torment.

Sandrin: But I thought-

Lilthra: There's a singleness of purpose to Anger that is too easy to blow in and out in any circumstance. Sloth is all wrong for Elizabeth, she's way too driven by her parent's ideals, and Greed?
(Thinking) Greed is so outdated in modern life that it might as well be one of the seven virtues. What's the point of capturing a soul if they don't even believe what they are doing is wrong!
(Excitedly) But Gluttony... aye there's a cured meat worth carving. Isn't it Sandrin?!
(Whispers conspiratorially with an unholy glee) Many people feel Gluttony is an inordinate desire to consume more than that which one requires, and sure that's one of the traditional definitions, but the modern day is simply *filled* with miracles. As the brothers scratched off fleas in their musty old monasteries, certainly they couldn't conceive of the present day.
(Victoriously) The stage is set. The field's already ripe for harvest. Modern fashion. Media. Fifteen year old rockers and teen TV stars removing their ribs and sucking marrow out of their hips. Pick any woman's magazine. Grab some hip huggers. *(ferociously)* The world is coming up long stemmed roses Baby, and the petals are T-H-I-N.
(Pause)

VFX: *Lilthra inhales and exhales.*
The cool thing is its a roller coaster ride where the greatest thrill is the tracks are out, but everyone wants to get on anyway. All it takes is a whisper here and there. Remember? Amy Murphy. 'She's cute and thin.' Then Danny? He dropped her because they didn't do the deed. Maybe she wasn't cute enough.
(Evilly) Maybe she needed to be thinner. And now, when she thought she could use some money to pay for the residence at university, the Modeling came at the perfect time.
(Innocent whisper) Who could have imagined that it would dredge up so many feelings of inadequacy.

Sandrin: You did.

Lilthra: Actually.. it was more of a rhetorical question.

VFX: *Sandrin's voice echo deadens and attenuates to approximate the voice inside Elizabeth's head.*
Sandrin: It just feels dark right now, because everybody feels like this some time or another. Don't give in to doubt.

VFX: *Lilthria's voice echo deadens and attenuates to approximate the voice inside Elizabeth's head.*
Lilthra: Who are you kidding girl? Just look in the mirror. Who's going to love you like that?

VFX: *Sandrin's voice echo deadens and attenuates to approximate the voice inside Elizabeth's head.*
Sandrin: Your family loves you. You don't have to feel this way. Pray for guidance. He will hear you. God loves you.

VFX: *Lilthra's voice echo deadens and attenuates to approximate the voice inside Elizabeth's head.*
Lilthra: Why should you bother God with such pathetic problems. There are thousands dying in Africa right now. What does God care about a fat chick with a big nose. Danny liked you and you screwed it up. Then he told everyone you were stuck up. No one wanted to date you.

VFX: *Sandrin's voice echo deadens and attenuates to approximate the voice inside Elizabeth's head.*
Sandrin: No..

VFX: *Lilthra's voice echo deadens and attenuates to approximate the voice inside Elizabeth's head.*

Lilthra: Frigid. That's what you are. Well, melt the ice. The modeling agency will take you. But, you can't go looking like this.

SFX: Elizabeth runs to the toilet.
VFX: Sandrin's voice echo deadens and attenuates to approximate the voice inside Elizabeth's head.
Sandrin: Don't give in. Just sleep on it. One night can't hurt. Just...

SFX: Elizabeth sticks her finger down her throat and retches throwing up in the bowl.

Lilthra: *(Kindly)* Don't take it so hard.
(Silence)
 Hey.. you won the first three rounds.

(More silence)
You were just due. Just get back on the-

Sandrin: -Don't talk to me.

Lilthra: *(Gently)* Sandrin.. I don't like to see you like this. Remember, I've done this before. You're liable to have a bumpy ride. Did you think it would all go easy?

Sandrin: *(Stunned)* I never thought that little Elizabeth would be hovered over the toilet vomiting out the remains of a salad.

Lilthra: *(Lightly)* Hey.. its college. Kids do stupid things in college. Don't let it get to you. Sure. You'll straighten her out soon enough.

Sandrin: Don't patronize me!

Lilthra: *(Taken aback)* Sorry..

Sandrin: If I had only not walked about with rose coloured glasses. If I came better prepared-

Lilthra: How long did you train?

Sandrin: Eight thousand, four hundred and thirty-seven years.

Lilthra: They *are* pretty complex creatures...

Sandrin: *(Disheartened)* His grandest creations.

Lilthra: That they are... but now you can see that field work is important. All that time in the classroom is never going to replace real experience.

Sandrin: I will *not* be caught again.

Lilthra: That's the spirit!.. And I wouldn't worry about wearing rose coloured glasses. The things is, how does anyone know if they are NOT wearing rose coloured glasses. Even if you think you pull them off, it could be just another pair right on your nose. When all you do is see through them, then there's no way to tell. For example if all I knew was rose colour because that's all my experience was, how could I ever even really know the colour blue when I saw it?

Sandrin: I have to go.

Lilthra: Of course. Take care.... Still friends right?

Sandrin: Never again. I will not be so easily fooled again.

Scene 5: Late Night at Elizabeth's Dorm.
Elizabeth is surrounded by papers, books, empty bottles and post-it notes. She's frazzled. Too little food and too little sleep has worn away the studious person she was. She has not called her parents or gone to class in weeks.

SFX: *Lightning bolt strikes and Sandrin and Lilthra are in Elizabeth's bedroom in her dorm. Papers crinkle as Elizabeth struggles to find a comfortable position to sleep and not think.*

Lilthra: Back so soon? What's it been?

Sandrin: Eight months.

Lilthra: I have this theory.

Sandrin: *(Deadpan)* Yes?

Lilthra: Are you alright Sandrin? You look absolutely stuffy.

Sandrin: You said you had a theory?

Lilthra: Oh.. I get it.. all business. You're not still angry about the little cleaning of her stomach last time, are you?

Sandrin: Your theory?

Lilthra: OK Sandrin, if you're going to be like that, I won't tell you.

Sandrin: As you wish. Elizabeth is going through a crisis of consc-

Lilthra: - OK... So pry it out of me already. Here's the thing. I have this theory.

Sandrin: So you said.

Lilthra: Human beings go through spiritual crisis, just like the lunar tides.

Sandrin: They happen with the moon?

Lilthra: No.. they go through them LIKE the tides. But just LIKE the tides you can pretty much gauge them. Like here for example. Elizabeth is going through a rough time.

Sandrin: Yes.

Lilthra: No need to get into why. We all know who deserves the pat on the back for that one. However, this is not unusual. As soon as a human gets a taste of free will, they may dip their toe in, or they may jump in with both feet... either way, they end up getting real wet. And as soon as you have free will, you begin asking "Am I doing the right thing?" "What should I do now?" etc.. etc.. Right?

Sandrin: This is not new information.

Lilthra: *(Gesturing for Sandrin to go along with her)* Riiiight?

Sandrin: *(Reluctantly)* Right.

Lilthra: What's especially interesting though, is that this flurry of free will inevitably ends. Someone finds pretty much their stride in where they are, and splickety-lick they make decisions and deal with unknown situations at a measured pace again.. until ... BOOM.

Sandrin: Boom?

Lilthra: *(Excitedly)* Boom! They're in university! And then it happens all over again. Oh, look! "There's new people to judge me!" "There's a thousand people I see every day and none of them know me!" "Should I be the old me or should I take on a new personality?" "The old me I know... but its so high-school.. but what if I do something wrong?" And then a whole rapid series of free will is exercised and a new wave of spiritual crises comes whooshing in.

Sandrin: OK.

Lilthra: And then the waters subside. You know who you are, but the next thing you know... *(Snaps fingers)* you're out in the world and you're looking for a job and woooosh.. the tide comes in. And it happens again and again through life. Marriage, children, grandchildren, retirement, even death. The waters rise and subside.

Sandrin: And that is your theory.

Lilthra: *(Proudly)* That's my theory..

(Pause)

You know the best thing about that?

Sandrin: What?

Lilthra: If there were no tides, you'd never find stuff on shore.

Sandrin: Stuff?

Lilthra: Yeah.. you know... treasures. Different coloured rocks, starfish, hermit crabs, oysters with pearls in them. If we didn't have tides, we'd never know what was beneath the waves- even how deep they were.

(Silence and a long pause searching for words.)

Soooooo... Liz is going through a spiritual conundrum. Asking herself the whole purpose of everything?

Sandrin: She's riddled with guilt. On one hand she is still obsessed with trying to look thinner.

Lilthra: You have to admit she's doing well at that.

Sandrin: She is one hundred and three pounds.

Lilthra: Well that's a start at least. Getting under that hundred pound mark would be a good goal.

Sandrin: *(Hiding his disgust)* On the other hand she feels terrible and tries to eat all the time.

Lilthra: Perfect. The old binge and purge technique. A classic among models; she's at least in good company.

Sandrin: She hasn't gone to class in weeks. Everyone she sees says she's too thin, so she stays in her dorm. Right now, she sleeps most of the time.

Lilthra: This is the brilliance of gluttony that most people miss out on.

Sandrin: Brilliance?

Lilthra: Sure. Most people think gluttony is stuffing your face until you tank out. But the truth is its more like Greed. You don't have to be wealthy to be greedy. You just have to love money for the sake of money. You don't have to be fat to be gluttonous, you just have to be obsessed with food. And you know what the best thing is?

Sandrin: I do not want to hear.

Lilthra: Oh, Sandrin.. stop taking this personally. This is not about you.

Sandrin: No.. but it is not about YOU either.

Lilthra: Well, I would beg to differ. I do well here, and its back to Dis for me full time. As I was saying though, the *best* thing is that she's still fighting it. She's not just falling demurely into darkness. What a testament to human courage! What an emblem of suffering and futility she is! Oh. I tell you Sandrin.. at times like this, I'm absolutely joyous.

Sandrin: I can't believe I...

Lilthra: Can't believe what?

Sandrin: Nothing.

Lilthra: No.. you were about to say something..

Sandrin: No. It is just. I could not imagine taking such personal enjoyment in someone else's misery.

Lilthra: Oh, get off the tree Sandrin.. the being nailed to the cross thing has been done to death! Elizabeth made the choice. Not you and certainly not I. Don't tell me you wouldn't be pleased if she listened to your advice. You just hate losing.

Sandrin: You keep assuming I have an ego in this, Lilthra.

Lilthra: *(Demurely)* You can't blame a girl for trying now can you?

(Pause)

You know what the trouble with you is Sandrin?

Sandrin: I have no troubles.

Lilthra: You don't know how to have fun. You can't even tell a joke.

Sandrin: This is hardly the time-

Lilthra: Not that I blame you. Humour DOES come from our side of the street.

Sandrin: From Hell? I don't think so.

Lilthra: Not that God didn't commit his own cosmic jokes, I mean the dodo, radishes, the Alliance party?

Sandrin: Now wait a minute.. what's wrong with radishes?

Lilthra: That's not the point.. Humour is based on offending someone or some group. Blondes, Newfies, the Pope, Dead Babies...

Sandrin: Dead Babies? How do you offend dead babies?

Lilthra: Yes.. for instance how many dead babies does it take-

Sandrin: I don't want to hear it.

Lilthra: Ok, let's take another example. When is a Jewish fetus viable?

Sandrin: I don't know.

Lilthra: After it graduates from medical school.

Sandrin: I don't get it.

Lilthra: See what I mean. Good jokes are always from our Father Below.

Sandrin: *(Distracted)* She looks completely eaten away.

Lilthra: *(Sadly)* We do not harm others a fraction of what harm we wrest upon ourselves.

Sandrin: Shakespeare?

Lilthra: Uncle Scratch. He had a way with knowing the limits of human suffering. I got him a bloodstone watch for his retirement.

VFX: *Sandrin's voice echo deadens and attenuates to approximate the voice inside Elizabeth's head.*
Sandrin: Rest now. Tomorrow is a new day and you can start again.

Lilthra: Yes.. rest.

Sandrin: Are you not going to speak to her?

Lilthra: No need. I've said enough.

Sandrin: Indeed.

Lilthra: Look.. she's trying to sleep. She looks almost peaceful.. doesn't she?

Sandrin: I have watched her sleep before.

Lilthra: *(Bored)* Sounds real interesting...

Sandrin: Maybe when mortals lose themselves to sleep that is when they're the most vulnerable. And being vulnerable, all of us have an opportunity to be honest with ourselves- and in that honesty, God takes form.

Lilthra: Sandrin.. I believe you're really learning a lot down here.

Sandrin: Lilthra, I-

VFX: *Elizabeth's voice over.*
Elizabeth: *(Sitting up in bed. Awash with pain and regret)*
I can't do this anymore.

SFX: *Books and bottles fall on the floor as she staggers out of bed.*

Sandrin: *(Weakly)* No.

Lilthra: This can't be good.

VFX: *Elizabeth's voice over.*
Elizabeth: I can't go on. It hurts too much.

Lilthra: *(Dark triumphant pleasure)* You know what this means of course. Clarity of thought. She's come to a decision.

Sandrin: *(Choked)* No.. please Elizabeth.. Don't.

VFX: *Elizabeth's voice over.*
Elizabeth: Just... swallow the pills. And the pain will be gone.

Lilthra: Sandrin. Look at the bright side. You're done your first assignment. Think of it as a learning experience.. that always helps.

Sandrin: No!

VFX: *Elizabeth's voice over.*
SFX: *Glass of water pouring*

Elizabeth: *(Looking in the Mirror)*.. Just swallow them down.. just like candy... no one will even care.

Sandrin: I care!
VFX: *Sandrin's voice sounds in the same room with Elizabeth.*
(Sandrin phases out of non-existence to appear beside Elizabeth)
Elizabeth don't do this... please.

Lilthra: Sandrin! No! Unfair! She's mine!

Elizabeth: *(Shocked)* Who.. who are you?

Sandrin: That does not matter. What matters is that you are loved. *You* are important Elizabeth. You have friends and family who are worried about you. And if you leave them.. do you ever think they will be whole again?

Elizabeth: .. I.. I.. I don't know.

Lilthra: Sandrin, I warn you. Leave her be! She belongs to Hell now. You can do nothing!

Sandrin: *(Takes Elizabeth's hand)* Listen to me. Trust me. You will find love. One day you will marry, and have children of your own. But until then... you've got to enjoy life. Look around you.. is this the way you saw your life going?

Elizabeth: *(Crying)* No... I just... I don't know what to do... I don't know who to talk to..

SFX: *The phone picks up and he starts to dial. Sandrin hands her the receiver as it rings.*
Sandrin: Yes you do.

VFX: *Voice on the other end of the phone's receiver*
Voice on the Phone: Hello?.. Hello?....

Sandrin: Go on..

Elizabeth: *(Places the receiver to her ear)* Mom...? .. I know.. I'm sorry I haven't called.. Mom?.. Can you wait just a moment? *(To Sandrin)* Will.. will I see you again?

Sandrin: No... Just don't forget. Love is not lost if you believe yourself worthy of it.

Elizabeth: Are you.. are you.. an Angel?
(Sandrin fades into the ether.)

VFX: *Voice on the other end of the phone's receiver*
Voice on the Phone: Hello?.. Liz are you there?... Hello?....

Elizabeth: Hello Mom...? Yes... No... he's gone now. .. I don't know. It's not important right now. Mom? I'm sorry to call at supper time. No.. I know you're happy to take my call any time but.. Mom?.. *(Breaks out into tears)* Mom.. I need help...

Lilthra: *(Gently)* That was a noble thing you did just now.

Sandrin: What..? What's happening to my wings.

Lilthra: Don't worry.. you won't need them anymore.

Sandrin: I feel.. strange. What.. what is this.. what is this.. feeling?

Lilthra: Emptiness. You never quite get used to it.

Sandrin: *(Mournfully)* What's happening to me?

Lilthra: You're one of the fallen now, Sandrin.

Sandrin: *(Choked)* No.

Lilthra: It's my fault, I'm afraid.

Sandrin: Your fault?

Lilthra: Well, remember I told you about my falling out in Dis? I would never be allowed back in if I didn't succeed and succeed big.

Sandrin: But Elizabeth.

Lilthra: Elizabeth's soul wasn't what I was after. It was you.

Sandrin: No...

Lilthra: Fallen angels are highly regarded in Hell. You'll like it there. Well, not at first, but it grows on you.

Sandrin: Why?

Lilthra: You broke the rules Sandrin. Elizabeth's life was her own to have or to lose. But you got personally involved. I warned you, remember?

Sandrin: I just couldn't...

Lilthra: I know.

Sandrin: And now I'll never see Heaven again?

Lilthra: *(Takes his arm)* Now, don't be such a gloomy Gus. No one can predict the future, not even Him. You know what we say below?

Sandrin: What?

Lilthra: Hope springs infernal.
(Pause)
Don't worry.. we'll work on that sense of humour of yours. I like you, Sandrin. I really do.

Sandrin: Oh..

Lilthra: What?

Sandrin: Out the window. The Sun.

Lilthra: Yes...

Sandrin: It's just.. I never realized how beautiful the sun looks.. setting in the sky.

Lilthra: I know.

Epilogue:
Behind the scenes, our souls are engaged in an endless struggle. If all of us took the battle to the front lines and saw the glory that lies within us, would there be a need for Heaven or Hell? Until that time arrives, another soul is thrown out of paradise to wander the world a little wiser... in the Shadowlands.

Spin, Spin, Spin

There is a Land that's somewhere beyond the horizon. You may catch a glimpse of it, when the sun sets, or in the moments before dawn. It's the twilight that flickers at the edge of imagination. Somewhere between reality and fantasy. It's the place where monsters roam, and portals to other worlds wait in the back of a closet and in the crevices of your mind.
Welcome, to the Shadowlands....

Pete Beamer is a man caught between two states of being- On and Off. When turned on, Pete is a dynamo of energy, enthusiasm, and a testament to faith. When turned off, Pete is the perennial cynic and bitter snark. It's not hard to understand how he got that way. Finding meaning in a world where truth is only as potent as the next forty-second spot, might mean an installation of a dimmer switch for all the grades of character.
Illumination provided.. by the Shadowlands.

Scene 1: The "Midnight Curfew" Bar and Grill
A broken down little bar on a side street in the basement of an old building. Rudimentary furniture, and somewhat raunchy music playing in the background. Bellied up to the bar, Pete Beamer is trying to quietly drink his vodka tonic and ignore the other patrons around him.
Pete runs between two poles in life- enthused and jaded. Easily moved by changes in the wind around him, he is either wildly optimist or an embittered pessimist.

SFX: *Clinking of glass, back beat of bad eighties grunge rock.*
VFX: *Fading in.*
Female Bartender: Like my hair gets so *(thinking of the word)*... hot.

Male Customer: I know what you mean-- it's the heat.

Female Bartender: Exactly, like the heat. Exactly. I mean, I can't do anything with it.

Male Customer: Sticky heat...

Pete: Humid.

Male Customer: What?

Pete: Its the humidity.

Female Bartender: Right-- like he said-- humidity. My hair gets just so...

Male Customer: Hot.

SFX: *Pete lifts his drink. The ice clinks against the glass sides.*
Pete: *(Mumbles)* God help me..

Female Bartender: What?

Pete: Just admiring the full drink I've got to finish.

Female Bartender: Ya, you've been drinking that for an hour.. do you want another?

Pete: No.. I'm good... I can't guzzle for some reason.

Female Bartender: I have this fish...

Male Customer: What?

Female Bartender: You know, my fish... he's surrounded by algae... I can't figure out why he's still alive.

Male Customer: What's that got to do with anything?

Pete: Drinks like a fish.

Male Customer: What?

Pete: I said, "I don't guzzle," she thought about people who drink like fishes, and voila.

Male Customer: *(Light goes, albeit dimly)* Ohhh..

Pete: Yeah.

Female Bartender: Yeah, like 'connect the dots', OK?

Male Customer: Who can figure out what you think?

Female Bartender: Did you read that book I gave you?

Male Customer: No... I left it at your place.

Female Bartender: That one about women-- you know-- written by that like... trekkie. I can't believe you don't remember.

Male Customer: I'm telling you, I left it at your place.

Female Bartender: What the hell was it called?

Pete: "Men are from Quiknos *(pronounced: Cronus)*, Women are from Angel 1"

Female Bartender: Yeah! Did you read it? *(Looks to Pete)* He's like this huge trek geek, and he can't remember it.

Male Customer: Trekker.

Female Bartender: Whatever. *(Turns back to Pete to talk)* If it were like Seven of Nine flashing her spando-leotard, he'd be like Alex Trebeck, but because its an actual book... its not like he can read or anything. Did you read it?

Pete: Yeah, I read it. "Men are from Quiknos, Women are from Angel 1" *(Slight pause considering a diatribe)* Women, you know what the horrible truth is?

Female Bartender: What?

Pete: The book goes on about how woman need to find a young man to satisfy them.

Female Bartender: Yeah, cause we reach our sexual peak at like 40.

Pete: That's biology, and you can't argue with it.

Female Bartender: Exactly. See what I mean? Smart man.

Male Customer: *(Trying to re-insert himself in the conversation)* I'm younger than you.

Female Bartender: That ain't the point.

Pete: Nevertheless, it's wrong.

Female Bartender: What?

Male Customer: But you just said-

Pete: -That's the horrible truth. Women don't need younger men. Men belong with women 1/2 their age, and not the other way around.

Female Bartender: Yeah? Where do you get that from?

Pete: Women LOOK for security, men for a way to prove to themselves they're still youthful-- still have the "edge." So what's the opposite? .... OK, a woman who's twice a man's age has good sex if she gets him before he peaks at 18-- course she could get arrested if she gets him before-- and what can she expect afterwards when she wakes up in the morning...?

(Pause)

Female Bartender: More.. great sex?

Pete: Nope, adolescence. So she helps him through puberty which ends at about 40.. at which time he puts her in a home for some younger chick with anti-gravity breasts and a yen for sugar daddies.. and the whole vicious cycle begins again.

SFX: *Door opens to the Bar and Lynn walks towards the bar.*

So yeah.. all the middle aged housewives rah rah themselves when they see a celebrity actress gets herself a twenty-something lover...
Just be glad you're not the one trying to teach him how <u>not</u> to 'fart and blame the dog' for the NEXT twenty years.

Lynn Reiden is a 21 year old business marketing university student. Bright, energetic, and savvy, Lynn is interested in becoming the best in the marketing game. She has dark brown hair bobbed to her shoulders, and matching dark eyes that take in all around her. Although inexperienced, Lynn is certainly not naive.

Lynn: I'm looking for a Mr. Beamer.

Pete: I'm Pete Beamer.

Female Bartender: He's all yours.

SFX: *Moves back to the male customer.*
(Sarcastic laugh) Lucky girl.

VFX: Talking in the background

Lynn: Friend of yours?

SFX: *Pete finishes his drink and swallows. Glass hits the bar.*

Pete: Yeah, we go a long way back. Alma mater of this particular watered-down drink. You're looking for me?

Lynn: Yes, Mr. Beamer.

Pete: Pete, Mr. Beamer is somebody who invented a car.

Lynn: *(Smiling politely, but certainly not amused)* Cute, yes.. well... Pete. You've requested a student for co-op?

Pete: You were supposed to come in tomorrow.

Lynn: Yes, well I wanted to get a head start and meet you. Your answering machine said you'd be down here-

Pete: Lynn isn't it?

Lynn: Ms. Reiden actually.

Pete: Fine, Lynn. May I call you Lynn?

Lynn: Actually I prefer-

Pete: - What is your Master's thesis about?

Lynn: My thesis?

Pete: Sure.. you're a Master's student.. Master's students have thes-eye, whether they are in business economics or yodeling.

Lynn: It's still being worked out.

Pete: What's the rough draft.

Lynn: It's not even in that form-

Pete: -Working title. What's the working title?

Lynn: Economic Imperatives in a Transmigrational Global Climate.

Pete: *(Thinking)* I see.

Lynn: I told you it's-

Pete: No. It's good. So you're talking about how all the jobs are going to countries with less benefits, cheaper workers, and lax environmental standards.

Lynn: Actually, its about competitiveness in the marketplace.

Pete: Couldn't we save money if we just cut the minimum wage in half?

Lynn: Well, sure.. but the cost of living.

Pete: Cost of living'd go down, wouldn't it?

Lynn: Eventually, and perhaps we've got inflated wages right now, but-

Pete: -But in the meantime people wouldn't take too kindly to the cut in their wages. Especially not professionals or computer technicians.

Lynn: Do you always ask a question and then-

Pete: -finish sentences for people?

Lynn: Yes, it's very-

Pete: -annoying? Yes, I can see that. Only when I've had time to unwind with some drinks, and <u>never</u> with a client. Can I get you something?

Lynn: No, I think I should go.

Pete: Can I get you something to drink?

Lynn: They talk a lot about you-- the academic advisors.

Pete: Really, what do 'they' say?

Lynn: You're impossible. You go through three times as many co-op students than any other placing... and you're a sexist pig.

Pete: Then why are you here?

Lynn: I was just leaving.

Pete: No, I mean, why did you come in the first place?

Lynn: *(Sighs)* They also said you were brilliant. That if I could hack it with you, I'd learn more about marketing in one semester than I would through my entire degree.

Pete: Sounds like a good trade off... About that drink...

Lynn: No, thank-you. I mean, I appreciate your interest but I don't think this is gonna work...

Pete: Fair enough.. fair enough. May I ask you one question before you leave?

Lynn: OK...?

Pete: What do you want out of life?

Lynn: *(Taken aback)* I.. I... I don't understand the question.

Pete: Its pretty straight forward...

Lynn: But, I want so many things.

Pete: Not things.. I didn't ask what things you want in your life. I asked what <u>you</u> want out of life.

Lynn: A good job... ?

SFX: *Pulls out a bill wad. Puts down some bucks and slides out of his bar stool walking away.*
VFX: *Voice begins to fade as he walks away from Lynn.*

Pete: *(Laughs gently)* Well, at least you didn't say "love..."

SFX: *Door to the street opens and shuts leaving the music from the bar fading in the distance. Slow walking of Pete and Lynn through the near quiet streets. Only the odd car passing.*

Lynn: Well, what answer were you looking for?

SFX: *Walking stops as Pete turns to her.*

Pete: I'll make a deal with you. When you know the answer to that question, then you can take the rest of the semester off, never show up at my office again, and I'll give you a glowing grade for the whole co-op.

Lynn: You're kidding.

Pete: I never kid. *(Pause)* OK.. I'm kidding about that, I do kid. But right now I'm being serious. The offer stands. I know how busy it gets. You stick it out with me, only long enough to answer that one question to my satisfaction, and I'll give you a free pass to do whatever you like for the rest of the semester. Do we have a deal?

Lynn: I don't know.

Pete: It'd be a shame to have shown such moxie coming out here tonight-- a day before you were supposed to-- take the chance to meet me, and then just trundle back to square one only to find another placement, wouldn't it?

SFX: *Pause. Then Pete begins walking away. In a moment Lynn walks faster to catch up with him.*

Lynn: Weren't you meeting a client in the bar?

Pete: There? No, I always let people know where I am on my answering machine. You never know when a client MAY need to get a hold of me.

Lynn: Well, why are you leaving now ?

Pete: It's getting late, and you should be going home, unless you want to stop over at my place for a nightcap.

Lynn: I think I'll pass.

Pete: Suit yourself. I have a great view from my veranda, through to the valley.

Lynn: Tomorrow morning.

Pete: *(Nodding)* Tomorrow morning, of course.

Lynn: Nine o'clock sharp.

Pete: Nine o'clock sharp.

Lynn: Good night, Mr. Beamer.

Lynn goes to shake Pete's hand.

Pete: Your hand? Why Lynn... you're an old fashion gal I haven't kissed a-

Lynn: -Just the handshake, Mr. Beamer.

Pete: Just. The. Handshake. Of course... Good night.

MUSIC: *Transitional*

Scene 2: First Day
Pete Beamer's Office is elegant, professional, with a decor of stone facings, rubber plants and cacti. There is currently no secretary, nor a desk for one. A small selection of filing cabinets are built into the wall. A large desk at the end of the room has a laptop set atop it. A huge fish tank filled with exotic varieties, bubbles silently on the west side of the room, and the south wall is a series of windows looking out to the harbour.

SFX: *Keys rattling in a lock. A moment's pause and then the outer door opens tentatively.*
VFX: *Lynn's voice fades in as she walks into the office. She calls back down the hall.*

Lynn: *(Calling to the Superintendent)* Thanks! I really appreciate this. He should be here by now.
　　　(Mumbling to herself) OK, Mr. Pete Beamer, its now 9:05.

SFX: *Light switch turns on. Door closes behind her.*
(Impressed as she comes in) Wow... <u>some</u> place...

SFX: *Walks over the marble floor, her shoes clicking. She comes closer to the fish tank. The pump bubbles and hums. She taps the glass.*

(Talking to the fish) You're quite the beauty. And you have friends, don't you?
(Pause) So... what do you think of Beamer? I mean.. he feeds you so you have to like him. But, other than that.
(Pause) Italian marble flooring. Stone facings on every surface... and look at the tank he bought for you. You could fit a diver in there....
(Longer pause) Not talking, huh? I don't blame you. You may not be piranha, but why bite the hand that feeds-

Two typically nondescript government agents (they could be male or female) and one 'Kill Cancer Today Society'

Lobbyist stand inside the door. Their voices calling from the other side of the room. G-man #1 is circumspect, almost quiet sounding. G-man #2's voice is nervous and pinched, racing at times to get to the end of the sentence. Cancer Lady is dedicated and serious about her work.

VFX: *From the other side of the room.*
G-man #1: -Excuse me?

SFX: *Turning from the tank. Tank noises fade into the background.*
Lynn: Y-yes.. Sorry.. may I help you?

G-man #2: *(Spoken quickly)* We're looking for the office of Mr. Peter Beamer.

Lynn: *(Spontaneous laughter)* You've found it.

G-man #1: Something funny miss?

Lynn: No.. sorry.. *(still giggling somewhat)*.. It's just the name- 'Peter Beamer.' That's the first time I've heard him called Peter.

G-man #2: You new here?

Lynn: Yes.. that is to say, I'm his new assistant. Please, come in, Mr. Beamer hasn't arrived yet. Is he expecting you?

Cancer Lady: No.. nevertheless, I'm certain he will want to speak with us.

Lynn: Please come in.. there are seats over by his desk. Can I offer you something? I might be able to rustle up some coffee...?

Cancer Lady: *(Quickly)* No, thank-you.

G-man #2: *(Even faster)* No.

(Pause as the other's look expectantly at him. Obviously he wants coffee but he's being silently pressured against it.)
G-man #1: Err.. thank-you.... but no.

SFX: *They all take their seats. Lynn feeling odd one out sits behind Pete's desk.*

(Uncomfortable long silence)
Lynn: You're sure I can't get you something? It's no trouble...?

(Responses are given rapidly one after another. Cancer Lady interrupting G-man #1's waffling.)
G-man #1: Well-

Cancer Lady: -No.

G-man #2: No.

Lynn: Alright then, well... as I said. Mr. Beamer is expect-

SFX: *Door opens quickly as Peter enters.*

Pete: -Good morning everyone!

Lynn: *(Aside to Peter)* Mr. Beamer... I thought you were going to be here at nine o'clock sharp.

SFX: *Hangs his coat and places his briefcase on the floor.*
Pete: *(Aside to Lynn)* No.. you said you were going to be here a nine o'clock sharp, I just agreed with you. *(To his guests)* Good morning! I'm Peter Beamer-

Lynn: *(Stifled snickering)*

Pete: *(Looking at Lynn as if he's missed the joke, and he has)* - and while I only recently have my new assistant, I'm certain I would remember if I booked an appointment first thing this morning.

Cancer Lady: Our apologies Mr. Beamer, however time is of the essence.

Pete: Then please, sit down. Lynn could get you some coff-

Lynn: -Already offered.

SFX: *Moving papers on his desk and sitting on the corner of it facing the three visitors.*

Pete: *(Smiling politely)* Then how may I help you?

G-man #1: Your reputation proceeds you, Mr. Beamer. It is said you could sell sand to Iraqis.

Pete: Actually, the product was technically called American Beach particulates. Apparently, sand made in the US of A has a more "land of the free" nature... *(Quietly, with false modesty)* and it was to the Saudi Arabians-

G-man #2: -Nevertheless, we have a challenge for even your marketing skills.

Pete: OK, I'm listening.

Cancer Lady: Do you smoke Mr. Beamer?

Pete: I'm sorry, they don't let you smoke in this building. I've argued with the superintendent enough-- something about a stupid municipal regulation.

Cancer Lady: That's not what I meant. I'm not asking you for a cigarette, Mr. Beamer. I'm asking if you smoke.

Pete: Occasionally, but not as a rule.

SFX: Stands out of her chair.

Cancer Lady: I'm afraid this won't work.

G-man #2: *(To Cancer Lady)* Sit down, please.

Cancer Lady: *(Aside to G-man #2)* You heard him, he smokes. *(Looking at Pete unblinking)* I don't want a smoker as our spokesperson.

G-man #1: It is a good thing then, that it is the government's money that's paying for the marketing, and not 'Kill Cancer Today.'

Pete: *(Politely inserting himself between the two)* I'm sorry, I think I've skipped a page or two.

Cancer Lady: How current are you on your politics, Mr. Beamer?

Pete: Politicians are expert marketers and impressive liars. How current do I need to be?

G-man #1: Three weeks ago the government passed the annual budget for the next year, three months early.

Pete: Yes.. I read something on that. Unusual, since we're barely into fourth quarter.

G-man #2: *(Proudly)* Government efficiency for you.

Pete: *(Unfazed)* Undoubtedly.

Cancer Lady: What wasn't widely reported, and frankly mostly ignored, that to do so, the government made certain... *(thinking)* compromises with lobbying groups and the official opposition to get their budget through.

Pete: Sounds like business as usual. How does this involve me?

Cancer Lady: Underneath the budget... another bill was passed. One that will change the tobacco industry in this country forever, and may end the scourge of cancer their cigarettes-

G-man #1: *(Interrupting her rising sermon)* - A new change in the smoking laws will require an extensive PR campaign, and we think you're the man for the job.

SFX: *Leaning back in his chair slightly.*
Pete: You want me to sell a new smoking law to the public? Isn't that something for the Health department to take on?

G-man #2: Normally, yes.. but there are some additional concerns that could be called into question if we did this 'in-house.'

Lynn: Additional concerns?

Pete: *(Turning to explain to Lynn)* If they do it, it'll look bad on the government. If they get a private firm to do the PR, it looks like industry supports the government's bid.. especially if we're not an NGO attached to anti-smoking campaigns.

Lynn: *(Becoming clearer)* Ahh...

G-man #1: The thing is, off the record-

Pete: -Of course, off the record-

G-man #1: *(Pause)* -Off the record, Mr. Beamer, the government never expected the bill to pass. We made the attempt-- to get the budget through-- however, recently-

G-man #2: -Thanks to some redefinition of civil liberties due to terrorist attacks-

G-man #1: *(Nodding his head in agreement)* -Thanks to some redefined civil liberty laws due to terrorist attacks, the government has the ability to put in place rather... *(Searching for the right word)* ... "stringent" nonsmoking policies.

Pete: *(Laughing softly)* What...? Are you removing health care from smokers? Hiking their insurance rates further? Tattooing "smoker" on their foreheads?

G-man #1: Noooo..

G-man #2: *(Aside and under his breath)* Shot down in committee.

Cancer Lady: Cigarettes will still be available at all stores as before.

G-man #2: At competitive prices to stop smuggling and aid in taxes.

G-man #1: With a slight addition.

Pete: What addition?

Cancer Lady: Each cigarette will be manufactured with a bio-electric patch.

Pete: A what?

G-man #1: A bio-electric patch. It's the latest technology. It activates when you take a hit, drawing smoke into your lungs.

Pete: You're kidding.

Cancer Lady: Not at all. The patch gives off 30 volts. Not enough to permanently damage the smoker, but it will give them a heck of a sting every time they suck in the tobacco.

Lynn: You're kidding.

Pete: What about rolling papers?

G-man #2: On some products its attached to the filter, rolling papers have the patch affixed to the papers themselves. Its extremely thin, almost like an onion skin, incredibly porous. Most tests show that smokers can't even tell the difference between the old and the new...

Pete: *(Mumbles)* You've already done experiments...

Lynn: ...until they draw it in.

G-man #1: Until... they.. draw.. it in... Yes, well, that's where you come in Mr. Beamer. Like I said, the government didn't expect the bill to pass, but now that it has. We must honour our obligations.

Cancer Lady: It's the decent thing to do.

G-man #2: Our esteemed colleague from 'Kill Cancer Now Society' is, as you can guess, anxious to see this taken care of immediately. The changes to the cigarettes are expected to be in the stores before the end of the year.

Pete: And you want me to...?

G-man #1: We need you to sell this to the public, Mr. Beamer. We know nonsmokers will have a hay day with this news, but smokers...

Pete: Are voters too-

G-man #2: We need someone with marketing savvy to make this work.

Lynn: This is unbeliev-

Pete: -Lynn.

Lynn: But Mr. Beam-

Pete: -Why don't you help our guests to the door.

Lynn: Yes, sir.

(Pete and Lynn are herding the three out of his office. Dialogue becomes more hurried as they get closer to the door.)

Cancer Lady: This is important work, Mr. Beamer.

G-man #2: And you came highly recommended. You're work on the portable battery charger alone-

G-man #1: -I wouldn't so quickly dismiss-

Pete: -You misunderstand me. If this campaign needs to be in place well before Christmas I'll get working today on it.

Lynn: But... you can't...

G-man #1: There is the matter of your fee.

Pete: I will send you a quote by the end of the business day.

G-man #2: That would be satisfactory.

Pete: I think you'll find the quote equally so.

Lynn: But-

Cancer Lady: - Thank-you Mr. Beamer. There are thousands of people in cancer wards now, who if they had this patch, might have quit smoking and saved-

Pete: -Yes.. well if we all only knew then what we know now.. right?

G-man #2: We'll look forward to that quote.

Pete: Yes and thank-you. Have a great day!

SFX: *Door shuts*

(Silence for a moment as Pete leans against the door thinking.)

Lynn: You can't seriously want to take this job.

Pete: Why not?

Lynn: It's a crazy idea.

Pete: Do you know who they were?

Lynn: Yes-- the government-- and some anti-smoking lobbyist it seems.

Pete: And you're surprised its crazy?

Lynn: But you'll be universally hated.

Pete: Then I'd better come up with a good promotion.

Lynn: You could just give it to someone else.

Pete: What fun would that be?

MUSICAL *transition*

Scene 3: Ideas, Ideas, Ideas
Pete's Office. Pete is pacing the floor, and Lynn is sitting on a chair taking down his ideas in her laptop.

Pete: Where were we?

Lynn: You cancelled the "Shocking Health Matters" idea. Nixed the campaign for "Every Breath You Take" *(Under her breath)* I told you Sting wouldn't allow his song to be used for this.. *(Normal volume)* and naysaid the "Sit-down-lift-your-chin-while-we-fascist-bastards-slap-on-one-more-electrode-to-your-temple" project.

Pete: Actually, that last one wasn't an idea.. Just a little tension release.

Lynn: I kinda figured...

Pete: *(Tapping his head in thought)* Think-

Lynn: -You know-

Pete: -Think-

Lynn: -its been three days-

Pete: -Patience. *(Continues tapping)* Think...

Lynn: Aren't you getting concerned?

Pete: Toast!

Lynn: Toast?

Pete: Peter's Inverse Law of Marmalade Toast Dynamics

Lynn: What is that? And what's it got to--

Pete: The amount of times dropped marmalade toast will land right side up is inversely proportional to the amount of time you have available to clean it up.

Lynn: *(Not following)* Okaaaaaayyyyy...

Pete: Because we need an answer today, its going to elude us. All we have to do is think we have all the time in the world and an answer will come to us.

Lynn: Okay, how do we do that?

Pete: Change the subject.

Lynn: I-I ... to what?

Pete: I have these.. well... fantasies of you at night. It helps me sleep.

Lynn: *(Stunned)* Excuse me?

Pete: *(Nonplussed)* You don't have to write this down, it won't be useful for the promotion. I have these fantasies about you at night. You are of course, the way you are... in that kind of repressed way- yes just the way you're looking at me now.

Lynn: *(Getting offended)* Repressed?

Pete: *(Moving closer and talking softly)* Yes, the way you have your hair back like right now in that tight bun, and the glasses. You like conservative clothes, don't you?

(Stunned silence)

Don't be offended... I'm sure you're a very sensual person.. like I said the repressed conservative look works for my fantasies. I just have one question.

Lynn: *(Considering a sexual harassment charge)* And what would that be?

Pete: *(More quietly still)* How can your skin be ivory.. like fine porcelain, it really reflects the blue of your eyes.

Lynn: *(Quietly)* Mr. Beamer...

Pete: *(A whisper)* Yes, Lynn?

Lynn: *(Whispering back)* You're standing too close to me.

Pete: *(Swallowing and stepping back adjusting his tie and fumbling)* Yes, of course, that was entirely inappropriate, I apologize.

Lynn: I would think so.

Pete: It changed the subject, didn't it?

Lynn: Inappropriately so... you're going to have to stop doing that.

Pete: I know.. I apologize, I have a problem speaking out what's on my mind.

Lynn: As long as we're clear.

Pete: Absolutely.. Do you have any questions?

Lynn: About what?

Pete: Anything in the past three days.

Lynn: *(Clearing her throat)* Well... now that you mention it. There was something about a 'portable battery charger'?

Pete: Yes?

Lynn: That's one product I never came across in my research.

Pete: It was a small item that I did a promotion for.

Lynn: What's so unusual about a portable battery charger? Sounds like it would sell itself.

Pete: It used batteries to charge batteries.

Lynn: So you're saying it-

Pete: -Took batteries to charge batteries.

Lynn: But that's-

Pete: -pretty much defeating the purpose, yes I know.

Lynn: How many units-

Pete: Three million.

Lynn: You promised you wouldn't-

SFX: *Door opens in the background*

Pete: -finish your sentences anymore. Sorry, I'm nervous.

Standing just inside the office are the Tobacco Executive and Goon #1. Tobacco Executive is a small attractive Mexican woman, whose soft speaking, even dulcet tones are marked by her preference and understanding that all things go her way because she is kind. And if they do not, they go her way because of Goon #1. Goon #1 is a typical enforcer. Large and thick both in musculature, accent, and intelligence.

Tobacco Executive: Señor Beamer... It is.. so delightful to make your acquaintance.

Pete: Hello?

Tobacco Executive: I am so sorry.. my associate and I have no appointment. We were hoping you might make some time for us, sí?

Goon #1: Sí.

Pete: Certainly.. please come in and have a seat.

Tobacco Executive: If you are having a particular private moment we could perhaps...

Lynn: No... please come in.

Pete: *(Disappointed slightly looking at Lynn)* No?

Lynn: *(Clearly but professionally to Pete)* No.

Pete: *(Back to Tobacco Executive, gesturing for his guests to sit)* There you have it.

SFX: *Pete sits in his desk chair. The other two sit before him.*

Tobacco Executive: Señor Beamer, I am but a humble employee of Rothlins International.

Lynn: *(Blurts out)* The tobacco company?

Tobacco Executive: Rothlins has many interests and products for the discriminating lifestyle.. but sí, our main line is cigarettes.

Pete: Yes.. I remember seeing a special about you on sixty minutes.

Tobacco Executive: *(Mock pout)* An unfortunate and skewed view of our company. Bad press I'm afraid is something of a cloud over our heads.

Pete: You have a way with imagery... *(Looking for her name)* Miss..?

Tobacco Executive: It has come to our attention that you represent the government in its latest attack upon our customers.

Pete: It has?

Tobacco Executive: *(Seductively)* And I am here to plead my case.

Pete: You are.

Tobacco Executive: Si, Señor Beamer.. You see we are simply trying to sell a product that our consumers enjoy. Certainly it may have some health risks, but.. *(Pause for the effect of the sexual innuendo)* what things most pleasurable in life aren't without a little risk.. sí?

Pete: *(Playing along)* Sí.

(Long silence.)
Lynn: Can I get you or your associate anything? Some coffee?

Tobacco Executive: *(Still locked eyes with Pete)* Coffee would be nice. What a delightful girl.

Pete: I've always thought so.

Lynn: *(Clearing her throat)*

Pete: *(Snapping back to the issue at hand)* However, you were saying about Rothlins?

Tobacco Executive: Of course, business before... pleasure. I respect that Mr. Beamer.. although I believe pleasure and business mix extremely well.

Pete: You have a proposal?

Tobacco Executive: Sí. Simply refuse to market this obscene law for the government and we would be happy to give you a lucrative promotional challenge of our own. Sí?

Pete: Yes, I see. Why- if I may be candid ?-

Tobacco Executive: -Oh, I so wish you would, Señor.

Pete: Why did Rothlins not fight and kill this bill before it was passed into law?

Tobacco Executive: I am embarrassed to express, Señor Beamer, to a man of such great intelligence and machismo as yourself, my failings... would you find me unattractive for such a mistake?

Pete: We all make mistakes.. *(Still rooting for a name)* Miss..?

Tobacco Executive: Sí, I missed the bill. We were steeped in the litigation of another unfortunate matter, and had-- how you say-- "Dropped the ball?" It is now Rothlins' intention to look into purchasing the star quarterback- your rugged self Señor, before true damage can be done to our fine line of products.

Pete: Are you saying Rothlins intends to defy the law?

Tobacco Executive: *(Mock pout again)* Señor Beamer, you astonish me. We are not monsters. We at Rothlins have always followed government sanctions no matter how draconian they are. Even now we are preparing our line for the changes to production to install the new "filters" as per regulation.

Pete: But if you are able to save the customer millions of dollars by effectively opposing a law-

Tobacco Executive: -We are able to pass the savings on to our customers. Vive la democracy.

Pete: *(Smiling)* Yes, Vive la democracy!

Tobacco Executive: So, we are in agreement, you and I?

Pete: And what will happened should I choose to reject this very generous offer?

Tobacco Executive: *(Deep sad resigned sigh)* Such a decision would break my heart, Señor. I like you... perhaps too much. You see, I am such a big fan of your work... ethic. *(Flat cold tone to Goon #1)* Pescados.

Goon #1: Sí.
SFX: *Goon #1 gets up and walks over to the fish tank. Tobacco Executive gets up and follows him quietly. Pete does not move.*

Tobacco Executive: *(Sweetly almost sadly)* Such miraculous animals fish are... are they not, Señor? In this tank they are so dependent upon certain conditions for life.

SFX: *Goon #1 puts his fist through the aquarium and the water, fish and assorted sand and fake kelp fall to*

the floor. Tobacco Executive and Goon #1 walk through the broken glass and water towards the exit.
Pete jumps up from his chair.

Tobacco Executive: *(Concerned)* How careless. My apologies, Señor Beamer. I will of course pay for any damage. Please, think on my offer.

VFX: *Voice fading as she walks out the door.*
... We never really consider how fragile things truly are.

SFX: *The door slams shut.*

Lynn: *(Trying not to sound frightened)* They.. they-

Pete: *(Nonplussed)* -Threatened us. Yes.

Lynn: Aren't you going to call the police?

SFX: *Pete walks to where the broken aquarium is and begins picking up the pieces on the floor.*

Pete: And tell them they broke our aquarium? They already promised to pay for it.

Lynn: Aren't you going to do anything?

Pete: I am... Why don't you find a bag and help me pick up the fish before they asphyxiate?

Lynn: *(Mumbling under her breath picking up glass)* Wonderful.. even fish breath their last against big tobacco.

MUSICAL *Transition*
SFX: *Fade Out*

Scene 4: Light Bulbs and Snow Shovels
Early morning. Pete's office. Floor is covered with a paint drop cloth. Pete is in overalls on a step ladder repainting the walls a burnt almond colour.

SFX: *Door to the office unlocks and opens. Lynn enters.*

Lynn: What are you doing?

Pete: I thought I'd give Da Vinci's cystine chapel a run for its money. *(A soft laugh)* What's it look like I'm doing? I'm painting.

Lynn: The entire office? The walls look...

Pete: Burnt almond.

Lynn: I would have said sienna sunset.

Pete: It certainly sounds more festive. I think a nice Mexican theme would enliven the place, don't you?

Lynn: Mr. Beamer... the proposal? Today's the deadline. If we don't have it in-

Pete: -Painting is always an opportunity to look at things from a new perspective. I like to redo my office at least seasonally.

Lynn: I thought that...

Pete: Yes?

Lynn: Well, the meeting with tobacco certainly motivated <u>me</u> to change where I live. But I was considering changing the location not a new paint job.

Pete: *(Feigning distraction)* I don't think I have the time to switch to clay tiles, but I think that would make all the difference in the world. Don't you?

Lynn: You're not concerned at all?

Pete: Sure, I am. *(Pause)* Though stone works with a Mexican theme, the colour's all wrong.

Lynn: Big Tobacco.

Pete: *(As if imparting wisdom)* The gutter calls to the sky.

Lynn: The gutter?

Pete: *(Gesturing to the wall)* Calls.. to the sky.

Lynn: *(Not understanding)* Of course.

Pete: When you're lying ass back on the ground, you can't help but yell at everything above you.

Lynn: I see...?

Pete: You certainly don't look at yourself.

Lynn: And we would be...?

Pete: The sky in this scenario. Rothlins isn't going to do anything. If they try to sue us, we're under contract from the government. We're just running a job. They were caught flatfooted, and now they need someone.. anyone to blame but themselves.

Lynn: Have you been here all night?

SFX: *Door opens and in walks Mariah Crowley. She stamps her feet on the mat before coming in further.*

Mariah Crowley has a distinctly southern Georgian accent. Her soft spoken voice is counterpointed with the absolute zeal she has for fitness.
At 32, Mariah is fit in all imaginable places. She is a woman fully in her prime, and fully aware of her capabilities. Owner of "Target Zero" Fitness Centers she has unstoppable faith in her charm, skill, and persuasiveness. Tall, lithe as an arrow, and unafraid to show her "curves," Mariah considers herself a triple threat- beauty, brains, and voracious business sense.

Mariah: Can y'all imagine? A snowstorm at the tail end of November. Feels like just yesterday we were worryin' the heat.

Pete: Mariah! Welcome.. commercial all done?

Mariah: Fresh off the presses.. brought it for your pretty blues to see. But I guess you're tied up?

Pete: This is my assistant, Lynn.

Lynn: Ms. Reiden.

Mariah: Actually, my name is Mariah... Crowley..

Lynn: No.. my name is Ms. Reiden.

Mariah: *(Looking at Pete)* I thought you said her name was-

Lynn: - It is.. it's just.. *(deep resigning sigh)* Lynn will be just fine.

Mariah: *(Confused)* Alrighty darlin' ... Do y'all have a DVD?

Pete: Sure... over by the fish tank. Second cupboard, there's one hooked up with a screen.

Lynn: I'll get it for you.

SFX: *Lynn opens the cupboard. Rolls out the shelving unit with the large screen TV and DVD.*

Mariah: Very efficient of you, Lynn. Just slide in the first track, won't you darlin'?

SFX: *DVD goes in player. Lynn clicks play on machine.*

Lynn: Be just a sec... Do you want the remote?

VFX: *Speakers for the TV begin pumping out the intro disclaimer to Mariah's DVD. Mariah talks overtop the announcer and hits fast forward.*

Announcer #1: MELT WEIGHT is a trademarked system from "Target Zero Fitness Centers." All people, events, ideas, and notions involved with this dramatization provide no basis to replace your normal exercise routine with--

Mariah: -That'd be nice, darlin'... I forgot about the legal-eagle stuff. Borin' if you ask me, however necessary. One sec.. almost done fast-forwardin' to our commercial.

Pete: I'm amazed you got this shot so quickly.

Mariah: Darlin', when you have a pip of an idea like what we cooked up together- waitin's just an excuse for missin' the boat! Sh! Here it is now...

MUSIC: *Melt Weight Theme music. Bouncy. Energizing. Modern Electronic.*

VFX: *Announcer #2, musical theme, and sound effects all coming from TV.*

Announcer #2: Why do most people drop out of health clubs across North America? How much knowledge do you have of advanced fitness equipment? What time of year do you gain the most weight? Feel out of shape? Feel out of motivation? No money. No time? NOW THIS WILL ALL CHANGE WITH <u>MELT WEIGHT</u>. <u>MELT WEIGHT</u> is based on time honoured proven techniques to get your heart rate up, work the entire spectrum of your muscles from ankles to quads. Use the <u>MELT WEIGHT</u> technique to get the full burn.

VFX: *Lynn and Pete whispering just in the background of the commercial*

Lynn: Aren't they just-

Pete: -Shh...

Announcer #2: You might think you can get this kind of workout at home... and you CAN. That's the beauty of the <u>MELT WEIGHT</u> full system workout. But for the best results, join your local mobile Target Zero fitness center! Our qualified personnel will assess you, help you design your personal <u>MELT WEIGHT</u> plan!

Testimonial Woman #1: I can't believe how easy and helpful my trainer is! She found a community where I could, "Get down to it!" And at a reasonable price! I don't even have to drive there! I meet the Target Zero fun mobile at the depot and I can be feeling full burn before my lunch break is done!

Announcer #2: Target Zero has convenient pickups all through the day, to fit YOUR schedule...

Testimonial Woman #2: I'm no different than any of my friends. I put most of my weight on during the winter months. I mean, with Thanksgiving, Christmas, New

Year's Eve, it's a license to pig out. Most outdoor fitness program require a summer routine, or a lot of equipment. Not MELT WEIGHT. I just get my Burn Buddy. It's the right fit for my height and build, and I'm meeting people. I mean actually meeting NEW people while I lose the flab. How great is that?

Announcer #2: The Burn Buddy is the LAST piece of exercise equipment you'll ever need. Toss away those bars, rolling or otherwise! Get rid of ab crunching forever! The Burn Buddy will have you rippling with muscles and slough off the holiday feast in no time! Made of solid factory plastic, and a traditional wood carving, the Burn Buddy looks attractive in any home! Long and slender, with a wide blade to give you control as to the weight burn you need. Burn Buddy is YOUR buddy in MELT WEIGHT.

Testimonial Man #1: What I love the most is that I can do all this and see new places. I mean, I've been looking for a fitness workout that gives me THIS much toning, AND a chance to see communities I don't have the time to see in my busy life. I used to hate the winter, now I can't WAIT to be outdoors! Thank-you MELT WEIGHT!

Announcer #2: Contact your Target Zero fitness centre today! Get to know your Zone Melt Weight Officer! They are READY to help YOU! Aren't you tired of being TIRED during the winter? Need a boost? Need to get back in shape once and for all? Let MELT WEIGHT run-off the fat from your body this winter! MELT WEIGHT will work for you. We guarantee it!

MUSIC: *Melt Weight Theme music ending.*

Announcer #1: *(In the Background)* Melt Weight is a program owned and certified by Target Zero Fitness

Centers. Target Zero Fitness Centers are indemnified from any actual results which may vary according to participant. Target Zero makes no claims as to the effectiveness or veracity of this or any of its other programs. Consult a doctor before involving yourself in any fitness program.
Melt Weight is a trademark, awesome product.

SFX: *DVD ejecting. Mariah removes it.*

Mariah: Well? What do y'all think?

(Pause)
Pete: Brilliant Mariah... It looks really flashy. I especially like the animation on the Burn Buddy.

Mariah: Thank you Pete.. we got that guy you recommended who drew the character for "L'il Stalin."

Pete: *(Nodding)* "The commie-cleaner who can." I remember.

Mariah: *(To Lynn)* And you darlin'? What do y'think?

Lynn: *(Trying to be diplomatic)* It's... rather unorthodox...

Pete: Mariah's a friend. She appreciates you being candid.

Lynn: *(Exploding out of her)* I can't believe it! You're selling snow shoveling!

Mariah: *(Correcting)* Snow shoveling with good technique, darlin'.

Lynn: It's still snow shoveling! I mean. You're "mobile" fitness centre is a large Winnebago with showers installed.

Mariah: A vista of visual delights.. community after community you've never seen before!

Lynn: And the "Burn Buddy?" I have two of them... one in my car if I get stuck on the road!

Mariah: No.. darlin'... you've got a snow shovel. A Burn Buddy is ergonomically designed and modified for high performance fitness.

Lynn: *(Dumbfounded)* What... what do you do if there's no snow?

Mariah: There's all kinds of cardio programs we've developed to use the Burn Buddy with. When the snow comes we consider those "high burn opportunities." In the meantime, we collect for neighbourhood watch as well as some extra coin for collateral community improvement.

Lynn: Collateral community improvement....?

Pete: Shoveling driveways.

Lynn: And people pay for this?

Mariah: I've got seven hundred memberships this month, and this new commercial ain't aired yet, honey.

Lynn: Wow.. I'm in the wrong business.

Mariah: Thing is darlin'... nobody's gonna use a snow shovel if they have to. You got to make the gain better than the loss. You can't go around shovelin' something down folk's throat.

Pete: Mariah! Say that again!

Mariah: What?

Pete: What you just said!

Mariah: You can't go shovelin' stuff down folk's throats?

Pete: Exactly! *(Kisses her excitedly)* Exactly! You're beautiful, Ms. Crowley! Beautiful!

Mariah: Why Pete, you gonna turn ma head.

Pete: Lynn, call up the G-men and my "best friend" from Kill Cancer Today. We've got a campaign!

MUSIC: Transition

Scene 5: Just Say Yes!
Pete's office. Drop cloth is removed. G-men #1 and #2 are sitting with Cancer Lady around Pete's desk.

MUSIC: Transition
VFX: *Voices fade in with Pete talking.*

Pete: Thank you for coming at such a short notice.

Cancer Lady: We <u>have</u> been waiting rather patiently for your new promotional ideas, Mr. Beamer.

G-man #1: The government is not a patient body.

Pete: With a four-year lifespan, I completely understand. Let me ask you something, gentlemen and lady, what's the biggest problem with selling your bio-electric patch to the consumer?

G-man #2: It hurts people.

Pete: Bingo! On the money...

SFX: *Sounds of a marker drawing on a flip chart board.*
G-man #1: *(Clears throat uncomfortably staring #2 down)*

G-man #2: *(Defensively)* Well it does... !

Pete: No... He's absolutely right. Mister..... *(Pauses waiting for the G-man to offer his name)*

G-man #1: Yes?

Pete: *(Giving up the attempt.)* .. Never mind.. As I was saying, he's right! It hurts folks. That's the whole point of it. To try and stop smokers from smoking. But of course the problem is, the stick doesn't work.

Cancer Lady: Stick?

Lynn: *(Helpfully)* Using a big stick to beat people into stopping smoking, instead of a carrot to encourage them away.

Cancer Lady: *(Understanding)* Ohhhh.

Pete: Exactly! Thank you Lynn. We use the carrot and the stick approach in marketing.

SFX: *Walking around his desk and sitting on the corner facing the others.*
With one hand, you draw the consumer hither, with the other you beat them away from what they think they want. It's a tried and true method. In fact I once knew a woman--

G-man #1: -We understand the concept. Please continue.

Pete: *(Disappointed at being interrupted but regaining his stride quickly)* Yes.. well, very well. In this case however, the carrot and stick approach is useless. Let's be honest. You've got a group of people who are so well fortified in their position, if they were in charge of Berlin, Germany would have won the war on D-Day.

Cancer Lady: I don't care much for the example...

Pete: And of course you'd be right. It was an unfair caricature. However, the metaphor holds. Smokers have had high prices, warning labels that stretch across their packages telling them they are partaking of absolute sewage with each puff. They have pictures of rotting teeth, diseased lungs, and aborted babies all in living colour across each cigarette deck. Has it stopped smoking?

G-man #2: No.

Pete: Has it lowered the amount of smokers?

G-man #2: Not really.

Pete: Not really. Smoking contains more than 400 toxins, 4,000 chemical compounds, tar, carbon monoxide. Smokers live on average 7-8 years shorter than nonsmokers and when they go with cancer it ain't a pretty sight!

Cancer Lady: All of this we know already.

Pete: Yes. You're right. You know this.. .but you don't know what this means. You think it means we need to reach smokers more effectively, and sure you're going to be able to stop some new smokers, and even some old smokers from lighting up. But... listen! We're talking about people who ingest poison every day, sometimes several times a day. Not only do they do it.. they're proud of it. They stand by their brand of poison!

Cancer Lady: So?!

SFX: *Getting off the desk and moving back to the flip chart.*
Pete: *(Quietly)* So, we don't TRY to save them. We don't TRY to shame them. We don't TRY to win them through arguments of health and their welfare.
                Instead we do this....

SFX: *Flips page on the chart.*

(Silence)

G-man #2: "Just Say Yes"...?

Pete: Yes.

G-man #1: Just Say Yes?

Pete: Yes!

Cancer Lady: *(Dumbfounded)* Just Say Yes....

Pete: YES! YES! "Just Say Yes!"

SFX: *Flips page on the chart.*
You've lived through the Reagan years of "Just Say No." Well, we're tired of being bullied around. You want to change the rules, go ahead. You want some crackpot out of control special interest group
(To Cancer Lady) --no offense--

Cancer Lady: Hey!

Pete: -To hi-jack our right to choose how we spend our money, how we live our life, what our leisure activities are?!

SFX: *Flips page on the chart.*
(Triumphantly) Bring it on! Bring it on! It will just be an extra <u>buzz</u>. Bring it on! We'll take this fascist legislation and smile.

SFX: *Flips page on the chart.*

JUST.
SAY.
YES!

G-man #1: It's brilliant.

G-man #2: We'll be heroes.

G-man #1: We'll be <u>folk</u> heroes.

Scene 6: Ear to the Ground
Tobacco Executive sitting in a dark office somewhere with Goon #1. They are listening to a "bug" that was planted in Pete's office.

VFX: *G-man #1's voice echoes through a weak speaker.*
SFX: *Knob turns the speaker down and then off.*

Tobacco Executive: So.. it seems our Señor Beamer has spurned my offer.

Goon #1: Sí.

Tobacco Executive: Unfortunately, a woman scorned is a sad and unpredictable affair.

Goon #1: Sí.

Tobacco Executive: I would never see harm come to such an artista.

Goon #1: Sí.

Tobacco Executive: His assistant however, looks so very fragile.

Goon #1: Sí.

MUSIC: *Transitional. Ominous!*

Scene 7: Drive By
Pete is walking with Lynn on the sidewalk. Light traffic is moving at a moderate speed along the street. Pete and Lynn are carrying paint and tile supplies.

SFX: *Moderate traffic passing by on the street lightly dusted with snow and slush. Gentle wind. Two sets of feet walking down pavement with snow.*
SFX: *Sounds of people shoveling snow.*
VFX: *Distant sound of aerobic workout.*
Lynn: I didn't really sign up to be your interior decorator.

Pete: Hey.. consider it a vacation from our work! We signed the Government. The promotion is in full swing for two weeks now. You can expect they will release the new campaign commercials before Santa's come and gone from town.

Lynn: Are you decorating the office after this?

Pete: A personal question, Lynn? *(Smiling)* I'm shocked...

Lynn: Actually, I just want to know if you're going to have me haul Christmas ornaments, lights, and a tree from the hardware store.

Pete: Well, it is just down the street. However, I don't celebrate Christmas.

Lynn: You don't celebrate Christmas? Why not?

Pete: Too commercial.

SFX: *Cross walk beeping sound for pedestrians to not cross.*
Lynn: You're kidding. Wait... don't cross yet. You almost missed the flashing don't walk.

SFX: *Shuffling boxes and bags in his hands.*
SFX: *A car speeds towards the intersection.*
Pete: And you think chivalry is dead. If you carried your share--
        (In alarm) LYNN! Look out!

SFX: *The boxes and bags are dropped on the snow covered street. Pete pushes Lynn hard. Her bags are thrown and she hits the side walk.*
SFX: *Car revs the engines and then hits the brakes.*
SFX: *Car crashes into Pete and he's thrown to the street.*
SFX: *Car speeds off into the distance.*

Lynn: PETE! Pete! Oh God! Someone call an ambulance! Pete! Pete! Help! Help! PLEASE!

Scene 8: Tidings of Joy
Lynn is walking up a snow covered walkway. There is no wind, but a couple of houses down, carolers are singing "Silent Night" in solemn harmony.

SFX: *Walking through snow walkway.*
SFX: *Sounds of more people shoveling snow.*
SFX: *Knocking on a door. After a moment locks turn, and the door opens.*
VFX: *Carolers singing "Silent Night" in the distance.*

Lynn: *(Quietly)* May I come in?

SFX: *Door opens further and Lynn enters.*
Everything looks very... tidy.
(Silence)
I know I shouldn't be here. I just... well... I'm sorry.

(Silence)
Say something!

Pete: Lynn, I didn't want you to come.

Lynn: I'm sorry. Why did you do that? Why did you push me away?

Pete: It doesn't matter. I just...

Lynn: What?

Pete: I just don't want you to see me like this...

Lynn: So you're in a wheelchair. You'll heal! It's only broken bones.

Pete: I know.. but you're looking at me with those puppy dog eyes, and well.. I don't want you feeling all bad because of what happened.

Lynn: Is that why you didn't let me in at the hospital?

Pete: *(Smiling)* Well, it doesn't matter now.. you're here. And look.. you're wearing your hair down.

Lynn: *(Stammering)* Well, yeah. It...

SFX: *Knock on the door.*
Pete: Hold that thought.

SFX: *Opens the Door.*
Melt Weight Shoveler: Clean your walk?

Pete: *(Smiling)* You're with Melt Weight.. aren't you?

Melt Weight Shoveler: Why yes! Have you heard of us?

Pete: *(Enthusiastically)* Yes, I have!

Melt Weight Shoveler: Great! So that will be 3 dollars for the walk and the driveway.

Pete: *(Still smiling)* Not interested.

SFX: *Slams the door shut.*

Lynn: *(Shocked)* PETE!

Pete: *(Pleased with himself)* I hate salesmen.

Lynn: Pete! I can't believe you did that! They're your client!

Pete: *(Smiling)* Not anymore. Time to put that promotion to bed.

Lynn: *(Soft gasp)*

Pete: *(Taking Lynn's hand and pulling her on his lap, grunting a little in the effort)* Come here.

Lynn: *(Concerned)* Your leg!

Pete: Yes, my leg is broken twice below the knee. My lap is just fine.

Lynn: *(Sighing softly at him)* Oh, Pete..

Pete: I have something for you.

Lynn: You have something for me?

Pete: Actually two things... *(Moans a little shifting)* .. If I can just reach...

Lynn: *(Concerned)* Let me get off-

Pete: Don't you dare. It took me two broken bones to get you here in the first place.

Lynn: *(Soft laugh)*

SFX: Unfolding a paper as he opens an envelope.
Pete: Here it is.

Lynn: A letter from Rothlins... the tobacco people? Those bastards... are they going to pay for running you down?

Pete: Now Lynn.. that was never proved.. look at the letter.

SFX: More unfolding of the paper.
Lynn: Mr. Beamer..... would like to present.... offer for.... Holy Crap.. do you know what this means?

Pete: You're right. Apparently the smoking campaign was so popular for them, they're opening up a whole new brand of cigarettes. "Jolt Smokes!" they are called. They want us to do the promotion. Apparently, the electro-patches after a while add to the stimulation of a cigarette

Lynn: Hooked on electricity...of all things.

Pete: Just another toxic cocktail to their mix. Whatever makes the customer happy.

Lynn: Wait a minute.. they want.. "us" to do the promotion?

Pete: Well sure... You don't think I can do this alone.

Lynn: Well....

Pete: The semester is over.. but I was hoping-

Lynn: *(Whispering softly close to his lips)* Actually, I think I've discovered what I want out of life.

Pete: *(Whispering back)* What's that?

Lynn: *(Even more softly)* Passion. I want to have the same passion for my life as you do.

Pete: *(Quietly)* So, what about the promotion?

Lynn: *(Quiet laugh)* As you say, "Sure sex sells, but how much does it pay?"

Pete: You know.. we're going to need to get to work on this right away.

Lynn: Uh-huh.. right away.

Pete: Nine o'clock sharp.

Lynn: Nine o'clock sharp.

Pete: And we may need to remodel the office after the holidays.

Lynn: Shut up and kiss me.

Pete: Just.. that other thing, Lynn.

Lynn: What is it, Pete?

Pete: Merry Christmas.

Lynn: *(Warm smile)* Merry Christmas, Pete. Merry Christmas.

They embrace.
MUSICAL: *Transitional and Fade Out*

Epilogue:
We are at our best as human beings when we let go of the images and fantasies that others market for us, and embrace the creativity within. Once we allow the honesty of our passion for people to set flight, lust and illusion dissolve, like phantoms into the landscape... of the Shadowlands.

The Seven Deadly Sins Part #5 - Anger: The Hitchhiker

The Hitchhiker was first recorded at CKDU 97.5 FM in Halifax on the 30th of October, 2003. The cast was as follows:

ARNOLD BECK	Logan How
TUCKER MACKLIN	Jeff Brown
OFFICER	Jack Ward
RADIO ANNOUNCER	Manfred Onward

Directors Jack Ward and Andrew Dorfman

Anger: The Hitchhiker

Prologue:
There is a Land that's somewhere beyond the horizon. You may catch a glimpse of it, when the sun sets, or in the moments before dawn. It's the twilight that flickers at the edge of imagination. Somewhere between reality and fantasy. It's the place where monsters roam, and portals to other worlds wait in the back of a closet and in the crevices of your mind.
Welcome, to the Shadowlands....
The scene is familiar. A car broken down on the side of the road, and a man... a quiet, unassuming hitchhiker is about to become an unlikely traveler down a snow covered road leading... to the Shadowlands.

Scene 1: The Pickup
A snowstorm rages and a man stands in the centre of a nearly deserted highway. Barely visible he waves frantically to get the attention of the vehicle that is approaching slowly. The hitchhiker is Arnold Beck. While he appears to be a meek, mild-mannered accountant, he carries within him a long repressed anger. The tire on his car blew up during this blizzard and he's miles from home. Arnold is concerned, wanting to get home soon so his wife is not upset with him.
In the pickup truck, slowly making its way toward Arnold, is Tucker Macklin. Tucker escaped from Penticton medium security prison four days ago. The authorities are looking for him, but he has stolen a pickup truck from a family that has gone on vacation. He's driving east and plans to dump the vehicle in the sea and take a ferry to the United States. Tucker is a crude thug and has a great disdain for what he considers to be the unfortunate circumstances of his life.

SFX: *Wild snowstorm*
VFX: *Arnold waving in the snowstorm.*
SFX: *Screech of unoiled pickup truck brakes and a window rolling down.*

Tucker: *(Furious)* What the fu-!!! What the hell?!?! Are you freakin' crazy?

(Arnold comes close to the driver's side door. Still speaking loudly over the wind.)
SFX: *Windshield wipers struggling. The car defroster roaring in the distance.*

Arnold: Thanks for stopping. My car has a flat -

Tucker: -Are you stupid?

Arnold: I'm sorry... I just -

Tucker: - It's a freakin' blizzard!

Arnold: I know.

Tucker: You can't stand in the middle of the road. Geezus!

Arnold: I know...

Tucker: I barely saw you, you goddamned, stupid, sonuva-

Arnold: - I know!

Tucker: What're you doin'?!

Arnold: My car broke down.

Tucker: Geezus... you gave me a heart attack. I don't need this sh- !

Arnold: -I know. I'm sorry. Can I get a lift?

(Pause)
Tucker: sure... I'll unlock the door.

SFX: *Leans over to the other side of the cab and unlocks the door, opening it with a squeak.*

Arnold: Back in a sec...
(Arnold walks away back into the storm, leaving Tucker alone.)

VFX: *Sticks his head out the window shouting in the storm*
Tucker: *(Confused)* Where are you going?

SFX: *Distant sound of a car door shutting in the storm*
VFX: *Slides his head back in the cab*

(Mumbling to himself) Stupid assed sonofa... Tucker... you don't need this sh-...

SFX: *Door squeaks a little more open. Arnold bangs is feet on the floor and sits in the cab shutting the door. Storm wind is muffled.*

Arnold: Sorry!

Tucker: What did ya - ?

SFX: *Pats his large old fashion leather doctor's bag and places it down by his feet*
Arnold: I had to get my case.

SFX: *Truck shifts into gear. Tucker puts the accelerator down and the wheels spin a little before catching traction. The engine roars as the wheels spin and then lowers to a normal speed.*
Tucker: You a doctor?

Arnold: Uh... no. Why?

Tucker: That bag's huge...

Arnold: Oh... of course. I forgot. It's an antique.

Tucker: There's room at your feet.

Arnold: It's OK. I'll just hold on to it for a while.

Tucker: Whatzamatter? You look like your best friend just stepped on your pet turtle.

Arnold: I'm fine.

Tucker: I only look like that when I'm halfway passed pissed town.

Arnold: I never lose my temper.

Tucker: No? You might try it sometime, you'll explode keeping it bottled up. Where ya headed?

Arnold: Just into Truro.

Tucker: I'm not going there, but I'll let you off at the city limits.

Arnold: That would be fine thank-you. My wife worries.

Tucker: Pussy whipped huh?

Arnold: I guess so.

Tucker: Never got leashed...

Arnold: No?

Tucker: Hell no.... *(Pause)* Really coming down isn't it?

Arnold: They're calling it the worst storm of the year.

Tucker: Hell of a time to be out working.

Arnold: Just driving back from the office at Amhearst.

(Pause)
What are you doing out on the roads?

Tucker: *(Annoyed)* None of your damned business.

Arnold: *(Slightly Nervously)* OK...

(Really long pause)

Tucker: Goddamned storm. Can't go any faster than 30. *(Pause)*

Arnold: I know... we haven't had a storm like this since I was a kid.

Tucker: You like the snow?

Arnold: Sure. I spent a lot of time in it. My Father didn't like us inside.

Tucker: No?

Arnold: No. 'Children should be seen and not heard.' He'd have a tough day... well, days.

Tucker: Yeah?

Arnold: Yeah.

Tucker: Well, I'm sure your Mommy did up your overcoat for you.

Arnold: No.

Tucker: No Mom, huh? Geez. Must have been real tough. I can see you're scarred for life.

Arnold: I'm sorry?

Tucker: *(Mumbles)* Goddamned... You know what the problem is with people like you?

Arnold: - Maybe I should have just waited with my car -

Tucker: -The problem with people like you is you have NO freakin' idea what real people go through.

Arnold: -But my cell phone was out of range.

Tucker: Yeah. My mistake. You understand completely. Cell phone huh? You drive a lot?

Arnold: Too much and not if I can help it.

Tucker: I like driving. It's like the only time I can really feel calm. You're in control when you drive. You know what I mean? Every other moment in my life I'm being bitched at by someone or other. I don't even get peace when I sleep... but when I'm drivin'....
(Pause)
Been across the country five times. In your car, you decide how comfortable you want it. You decide where you sleep. You decide when and what you eat. You decide what music to listen to. You're the master of your own friggin' destiny.

SFX: *Turns the ON/OFF switch for the radio, static squeals.*
Damned friggin' radio... can't get anything here.

Arnold: Power's out all across Halifax... something about a transformer blown.

SFX: *Spins the tuner dial getting more static*
Tucker: You'd think that one of these stations would come in.

Arnold: Not a lot on the AM band in these parts.

Tucker: FM button's broke.
(Disgusted muffled curse)
SFX: *Snaps off the radio*

Arnold: I usually listen to books on tape myself.

Tucker: Yeah? I guess you'd just be bench pressin' vocabulary all the way home by now, if your tire didn't blow.

Arnold: I guess.

Tucker: Didn't you have a spare?

Arnold: I... don't know how to change it.

Tucker: *(Laughing sarcastically)* Yeah? Well, those lug nuts can be hard to turn.

Arnold: I'm stronger than I look.

Tucker: Oh... you work out?

Arnold: Just good genes. I exercise... occasionally.

Tucker: I like a good a work out. Ya watch wrestling?

Arnold: I am not really into sports.

Tucker: *(Laughing)*... No... not Olympic wrestling. PRO... ya know? The real stuff. Big ass guys beatin' the snot out of each other. Not some pansy in a leotard groping another pansy on all fours.

Arnold: And it's real?

Tucker: I don't give a flying crap what anyone thinks. You don't see those Olympic fairies getting broken bones or dyin' in the ring do ya?

Arnold: Oh I see.

Tucker: Well?!

Arnold: No I guess not. I've never seen Pro wrestling... ah... shouldn't you be watching the road?

Tucker: Real wrestlers drive all over the country to wrestle too. They don't have gold buses like goddamned pansy kids on the back street, or some other bunch'a freaks.

Arnold: *(Nervously watching the road)* Yeah.. ?

Tucker: Yeah. And I remember this one story. There's Vincent Lopez the former world champion wrestler, the Butcher Vachon and the Mad Russian. They're all riding in the same car. The Russian's sleeping in the back seat, and Lopez is friggin' bored, right? He looks at the Butcher and says, "Follow my lead." Then he slams his hand on the car door, and skids on the brakes. The car squeals to a halt sideways on the road, and the Russian's wide awake now in the back-seat.

Arnold: I don't get -

Tucker: So Vince yells out. "I didn't see him! I didn't see him!" and he's screamin' like he's hit a cyclist!

Arnold: That's awful!

Tucker: *(Laughing)* It gets worse. So Vince tells 'em to wait in the car and he gets out and runs back to check on "the body." It's a real foggy night, and they can't see him and he makes some groaning sounds. *(Moans)* Oh!.. Ohh.. Oh!
The Russian freaks. He wants to call the police... Lopez comes back and reaches past the Butcher into the glove compartment. He grabs this gun and says,
"He's seen my face, I can't afford to get caught. So I'm gonna take care of him"
The Russian is beside himself. Vince walks back, empties the gun BLAM BLAM BLAM and comes back.

Arnold: I can't believe it.

Tucker: That ain't the half of it. So Lopez tells 'em that the dead cyclist has this expensive ring, but he can't get it off his finger. He rifles through the glove compartment and grabs this huge hunting knife and goes back to "chop" - oh hell.

Arnold: What's wrong?

Tucker: Gas station's closed. I wanted a coffee.

Arnold: We're getting low on gas too?

Tucker: Yeah, I've got some gas in a tank in the back.

Arnold: Really?

Tucker; Yeah, it's a long drive from Ontario...

Arnold: You're from Ontario?

Tucker: *(Angrily)* You're just breakin' out all over with a bad case of nosey.

Arnold: Sorry.

Tucker: Why don't you just mind your own damn business?

Arnold: Sorry... I just... well you said.... sorry.

Tucker: Gas costs a lot out here!

Arnold: I know.

Tucker: No frickin' crime bringin' your own gas, is it?

Arnold: I said I'm sorry... so... what happened with the cyclist?

Tucker: What?

Arnold: The fake cyclist... you know with those wrestlers.

Tucker: Nothin'... I don't want to talk about it. Just shut the hell up.

(Pause)

Arnold: Sorry.

Tucker: Yeah... let's give that word a break for a while, all right?

Arnold: Look... this is OK. You can stop right here. I'll go to the gas station, maybe get a pay phone and-

Tucker: Oh no. Oh no, no, no, no. You stood in front of MY truck, man. You wanted a ride. *(Pause)* So let's go for a ride.

Arnold: What? What do you mean?

Tucker: I mean, by the time we're done, you'll get in touch with your feelings.

(Silence)
(Dangerous laughter) And I won't even charge you for the therapy... how's that for a deal?

Arnold: I'd really rather -

Tucker: -Just sit back and enjoy... we'll be in Truro soon enough. Don't forget your wife?

Arnold: What... what about her?

Tucker: *(Dangerously)* She'd worry a whole lot more if you never turned up, wouldn't she?

Scene 2: Driving the Snowstorm

Tucker: You're awful quiet.

Arnold: You said -

Tucker: -Yeah, I know what I said. I'm beginning to think you're right. You just can't get pissed.

Arnold: Oh, I get angry.

Tucker: You said -

Arnold: - I said, "I never lose my temper" and I don't. I know exactly where it is.

Tucker: Ya, real funny.

Arnold: I wasn't joking.

Tucker: That's what makes it funny.

Arnold: You know what the problem is with people today?

Tucker: Folks like you who know "what the problem is with people today?"

Arnold: I'm so - Never mind.

Tucker: That's better. Did you just say "Never mind" 'cause I pissed you off? Or because you're scared of saying "sorry" to me again?

Arnold: I'm not scared.

Tucker: That's not an answer.
(Silence) OK... *(Sarcastically)* so I'm dyin' to know. What's the problem with people today?

Arnold: Lack of focus.

Tucker: Geezus. That's sublime. That's goddamn sublime. You're one of those goddamned prophets. Givin' tasty tidbits of popcorn wisdom from the Almighty. *(Silence)* So, how did you come by this revelation.

Arnold: *(Pauses contemplating)* You're just goin' to ridicule me.

Tucker: Not at all. I'm sittin' on the goddamned edge of my seat. Seriously, man. Tell me. We've got miles of the white crap in front of us and I'm learning the meaning of life. I've fulfilled the goals in my goddamned high-school yearbook. Don't stop now. You've still got to guess what I was voted "most likely to be."

(Pause)
Arnold: My father was a wise man.

Tucker: Most Dads' are.

Arnold: No... he was unique. He filled me with awe. I know most sons are pretty amazed by their fathers, but I was struck with awe.
(Pause)
Many times. Sometimes in the same night. My father had a thing about focus. He worked at the mines all day. I never thought anything of it.
He wanted to be a fiddler for a living.

Tucker: Fiddler?

Arnold: Yeah, you know... violinist? Play for square dances, kitchen ceileigh what have you. He'd play nearly every night.

Tucker: Oh... gotcha.

Arnold: Anyway. He was a lousy fiddler. He'd play until his fingers bled and never got any better. Thing is, it wasn't a real desire to do well that kept him practicing all night.

Tucker: No?

Arnold: No. It was anger. Pure anger. He got better eventually. Broke a lot of bows getting there. Focus in life... even your anger. See, I don't see a real value in just being angry with people. I put it into my work. It pushes me to better things. As much as Dad tried to focus it though... anger just pushed him down.

(Long pause)
SFX: Knob on the radio turns on and a squeal of static emits from the radio. Tucker turns the knob as it crackles down the dial.
Tucker: You like music?

Arnold: Sure... still not going to get much in.

SFX: Turns dial, a series of crackling interference and half stations. He pauses trying to get in a couple but nothing comes in well enough to really understand. .
Tucker: The aerial isn't much either.

SFX: Semi-intelligible news voice comes on. Tucker leaves it at the station.
VFX: Announcer's voice spotted with static.
Announcer: ... Padres continue to outpace the Mets in... 5th game in... stadium. Police are warning ..... no word on the highway murderer... until then.. the manhunt continues....
Stormy weather is.... hurricane force from offshore..... expect Tuesday we'll.... back in a minute with business from your all News station.. CKUD 99.3.

Arnold: That's probably your best bet. The News station is closest.

SFX: Turns off the radio.
Tucker: Naw... You know what song I liked when I was a kid?

Arnold: What?

Tucker: Big Rock Candy Mountain.

Arnold: Yeah. I remember that song.

Tucker: Ohh... the buzzzzzzzz-ing of the bees, in the cigarette trees, near the soda water fountain.

Arnold: And the lemonade springs where the bluebird sings...

Tucker and Arnold: In the Big Rock Candy Mountain...

Tucker: *(Laughing)* That's good... you know the verses?

Arnold: No... It's been too long.

Tucker: That's the thing about this song... it comes across like a kid's tune, but it's really for hobos. It's like a place they go when they die or something.

Arnold: Yeah?

Tucker: Well check this out..
(Sings) In the Big Rock Candy Mountain, The cops have wooden legs
The bulldogs all have rubber teeth, And the hens lay soft-boiled eggs
The farmer's trees are full of fruit, And the barns are full of hay
I'm bound to go, Where there ain't no snow

Where the sleet don't fall, And the winds don't blow
In the Big Rock Candy Mountain.

(Pause expectantly)
See what I mean?

Arnold: Yeah I can see that.

(Longer Pause)
Tucker: *(Sings to himself distantly)* In the Big Rock
Candy Mountain, The jails are made of tin.
You can slip right out again, As soon as they put you in.
There ain't no short-handled shovels, No axes, saws nor picks,
I'm bound to stay, Where you sleep all day,
Where they hung the jerk, That invented work
In the Big Rock Candy Mountain.
(Spoken)... yeah... the Big Rock Candy Mountain.

(Pause)
You read?

Arnold: Sure.

Tucker: Ya, You look like you read lots.

Arnold: Thanks.

Tucker: That's not exactly a compliment... dork.

Arnold: Oh.

Tucker: Don't get me wrong. I used to read a lot too... and then, well, you know things happen. TV takes up a lot of time you know.

Arnold: I don't really own a television.

Tucker: *(Laughs harshly)* Yeah I figured that. *(Looking for a fight)* You think you're better than me, or somethin'?

Arnold: No.

Tucker: You think you're like smarter or somethin' just 'cause you don't have a TV?

Arnold: I never said that.

Tucker: Well then what is it?

Arnold: I just... I just... don't have a television... It never appealed to me. You're right. I read a lot as a kid... that's all.

Tucker: I read a lot too you know.

Arnold: *(Trying to avoid a fight)* Alright.

Tucker: You read comics?

Arnold: Sure...

Tucker: I was just thinking how much I liked reading comics when I was a kid. I loved this comic book called Rom Spaceknight. He was just this guy in this tin suit and he couldn't get out of it. Ya heard of him?

Arnold: No... was he honourable?

Tucker: Honourable?

Arnold: Yes. I read about King Arthur's knights when I was young. They were all... honourable.

Tucker: Oh Christ ya. As honourable as they come. He had honour coming out his ass.

He'd chase all around the galaxy for these... these.. things called ah... um..
(Searching his memory for their name) the Dire Wraiths...

Arnold: Apt name for an antagonist.

Tucker: *(Pretending he knows what Arnold is talking about)* Yeah... that's what I thought too...
Anyway, He didn't kill anybody. He had this code about killing... You would have liked that...
Even though he was this spaceman he was like a knight...
(Laughs) I guess that was the whole point of "Rom... Spaceknight."

Arnold: Sounds like he was a hero.

Tucker: Yeah, but it wasn't that easy...

Arnold: Noble quests never are.

Tucker: He got stuck in the armor. Half cyborg like that 'Van-damn' flick. Half machine couldn't just be a man. He met this one chick named Brandy. And he really cared, you know? So much he'd give up being a spaceknight in a heartbeat to be a man for her.

Arnold: But a quest...

Tucker: Yeah I know it's corny, but I loved that stuff.

(Pause) Most kids read Batman, or Superman, or Spiderman or some shit like that. I'd just read Rom. Maybe it's like you said... something noble about the way he did stuff, you know? Pure. Innocent. Goddamned virtuous.

Arnold: Yes. I can see that.

Tucker: *(Laughs)* You know what the kicker is? I went on the web recently - you know... the Internet?

Arnold: Yeah..?

Tucker: I go looking for "Rom, Spaceknight." Found out the comic finished at issue 75 just like that bam!.
I guess they tried to make new Rom comics a couple of times but they couldn't. They didn't own the rights to Rom... never did.
Some toy company did...
Get this... they made a comic based on a single toy. Weird eh? Hell in the comics Rom's space armor always looked crappy.
But the toy Rom, it looked like shit. It looked like a tiny little trash bin with glowing eyes. No one bought it...
So as a toy, Rom's a failure... as a comic book hero he's popular, catch that?
So then, then I read about all these guys who like Rom the Spaceknight like me. They're pissed off because somewhere down the line they actually make a mini-series of comics called "Spaceknights" but in the first one... very first issue... they kill off Rom.... and every Rom fan freaks!
And it's not like he dies a hero. It's not even a good death, he just gets destroyed in the ship.
I never read this series... *(Disgusted)* "Spaceknights." Then there's an article interviewing the writer of this crap," Jim-who-gives-a-damn.
You know what he says about killing off Rom?

Arnold: No.

Tucker: He's all matter of fact, all balls of brass. He says, "I read Rom. I thought it was stupid... And I just really needed to make money to pay for my boat."

(Pause)

Arnold: There's no honour today. Nobody cares about what's right or wrong.

Tucker: *(Distantly)* Yeah... exactly. I just can't get it out of my head though. Here's something that starts off as a toy, fails miserably.
Then the comic book is just there to sell the toy it takes on... well... like a hero of old-

Arnold: -A legend.

Tucker: Yeah! That's it... a legend... for kids all over the place for like ten years. Then poof. It's gone.
And when it finally comes back. It makes money for some sonuvabitch who doesn't even like it.
Someone who just fixed his boat with the profits.
Money to legend to money. That's... well... that's... something...

Arnold: Irony.

Tucker: What?

Arnold: It's ironic. Failed to make money, and eventually did so only because it was popular not as merchandise. That's irony.

Tucker: Yeah? Well it's somethin' alright. So I did more reading and checked on the guy who originally wrote Rom, Spaceknight. He's a famous comic book writer back when I was a kid. But where is he now??
(Pause)
Poor bastard. Car accident. He's a vegetable.

Arnold: That's... that's too bad. I'm sorry.

Tucker: Worst way to go... At least Rom got blown away... Not stuck in a hospital somewhere...

Yeah... Better to die fighting shapeshifters than rot away.

Scene 3: Radio Report
SFX: *The radio knob turns on again, and the tuner turns bringing static. A couple of different music stations flutter in and out.*

Tucker: Damn radio... Can't even get one decent station... just one.

SFX: *Tunes the News station back in.*
VFX: *The Announcer's voice comes in and out rolling amidst a sea of static.*

Announcer: ... the CKUD 99.3, 7:35 News brief for.... explosion in the ... embassy in Saudi Arabia. 12 dead and 4 wounded. No group has yet claimed authority...
Tucker: *(Mumbles)* Goddamn Middle East. I'm telling ya.. Nuke the bastards...

Announcer: ... No word on highway slayings... police are saying that there is no connection.... of four different people on highways throughout... Tucker Macklin. Macklin escaped Penticton medium security prison eight days ago... Police believe he's headed East in-

SFX: *Radio snaps off.*

Arnold: I was listening to...

Tucker: Reception was giving me a headache.

Arnold: But they were talking about the escaped-

Tucker: -Yeah.

Arnold: *(Nervous laugh)* I just had the funniest thought.

Tucker: *(Dangerously)* Yeah?

Arnold: *(Picking up on the vibe)* Noth-nothing...

Tucker: *(Evilly)* No... please tell me. Mr. Friggin' Reader. What clever thought's runnin' through your head?

Arnold: It's... it's nothing really. Just... just wondered about that-

Tucker: -Yeah?

Arnold: About the wrestlers. You... you never finished the story.

Tucker: Oh yeah... *(Laughing at his uncomfortableness)* Yeah.. where was I?

Arnold: The Champion guy..

Tucker: Vincent Lopez.

Arnold: Yeah... yeah... Lopez. He pretended to shoot a cyclist, and took a knife... supposedly cut off his finger and got a ring.

Tucker: Yeah... That's right. So he comes back to the car a moment later.. His hand doused with fake blood - after all EVERY pro wrestler has a fake blood bottle on him. He shows his own ring up for both the Butcher and the Mad Russian to see. Pleased as punch that he's gonna get away with murder.

Arnold: *(Nervously trying to engage the conversation)* No one gets away with murder.

Tucker: The Russian's just livid! He didn't know WHAT to think! He's really this Spanish guy... his first time in America... on this H1 visa. He don't like the cops, and he's sitting in the car with a murderer. What's he supposed to do?

So Lopez.. *(Laughing)* ... the bastard... waits until the Butcher is sleeping in the front seat and leans back to the Russian and whispers, "I don't trust the Frenchman... We can't afford to be found out. We have to do away with him!"

Arnold: Unbelievable.

Tucker: Yeah... then they told the mad Russian at the next motel. He was pissed. But they all had a good laugh when it was over.
(Uncomfortable Pause)
So... YOU ever kill anyone?

(Short pause)
(Laughing).. You should see your face... white as a friggin' sheet.

Arnold: Yeah... *(nervous laugh)..* good one...

(Another pause)

Tucker: You want to know if I've killed someone?

Arnold: No.

Tucker: But that's what you're thinking... ain't it?

Arnold: No... I mean... I just thought.

Tucker: You just thought that maybe I was the guy from the manhunt... that Tucker Macklin guy?

Arnold: It was a stupid thought... you know. Long day... ride with a stranger... snowstorm....

Tucker: So what if I told you I was... ?

Arnold: I don't want to know.

Tucker: No? I didn't say I was, now did I? I just asked what you would do if I was.

Arnold: I... I... I don't know.

Tucker: Overpower me with your doctor's bag?

Arnold: No... of course not... there's -

Tucker: Yeah... you're pretty much not able to do anything are you?

Arnold: Look... I don't want to talk about this anymore.

Tucker: Why? What's the matter? I'm not <u>scaring</u> you am I?

Arnold: No... I just... I just... I don't want to talk about it, that's all.

Tucker: Shit.

SFX: Car starts to decelerate
Arnold: What?

Tucker: Lights up ahead... it's a roadblock or something.

Arnold: Maybe it's Truro?

Tucker: No... we're not there yet... only been 15 miles or so... See the flashing blue light?

SFX: Wipes the fog from the dashboard
Arnold: Yeah...

Tucker: Looks like a truck jackknifed... there's only one lane. We're coming up to a cop. *(Pause)* Be cool.

Arnold: I could get out here... the officer could-

Tucker: You're not going anywhere.

Arnold: What?

Tucker: You heard me. You're gonna sit there. And not make a sound.

Arnold: Wh- why?

Tucker: You're the brainiac... figure it out.

Arnold: You're not-

Tucker: That's right. No shit, Sherlock, you got it on the money before.

Arnold: Mack-

Tucker: -Macklin. Tucker Macklin... You'll notice handle's rusted out on your door. Don't try to run.

Arnold: How did you-?

Tucker: -I checked this truck out before I stole it. It's an old beater... and no one's going to know it's gone for at least another week. So keep cool.

Arnold: Oh God.

Tucker: Or I'll ring you're scrawny neck.

Arnold: Oh God...!

Tucker: We clear?

Arnold: Y-y-yes...

Tucker: Good... so shut the hell up. Or I'll kill you right here.

Scene 4: Accident
SFX: *Car inches forward and Tucker rolls down his window.*
SFX: *Wind howls and snow blows into the cab.*
VFX: *Officer's voice shouting over the wind.*

Officer: Where you folks headed?

Tucker: Evenin' Officer, nice night...

Officer: Yeah... right. Great night. It's a mess out here. Did you know the highway's closed?

Tucker: No sir, I did not.

Officer: How far are you headed?

Tucker: Friend and I are going to Truro.

Officer: Well... be careful. This tractor-trailer's not the only accident on the road. You shouldn't be out here...

Tucker: Only as long as we need to be sir... I promise.

Officer: Alrighty then... Sir?
VFX: *Leans in to speak to Arnold. Does not need to shout as much inside the cab.*

Arnold: Uh... yes.. Officer?

Officer: You... keep your friend awake and your eyes peeled. Snow's coming down so fast it's easy to lose the tracks and drive yourself right off the road.

(Pause)
Sir?... You alright?

Tucker: My buddy's just a little under the weather himself officer. Must be going around with the storm...

Officer: *(Hollow Laugh)* Right... under the weather.

Tucker: Don't worry though... We'll keep an 'eye' on each other... won't we?

Arnold: *(Terrified)* Uh... y-y-yeah... Sure.

Officer: You don't look so good, sir. Do you need an aspirin or something?

Arnold: I.. I...

Tucker: I think he just needs to lay down... don't you.. man?

Arnold: Yeah... sure.. I'll be alright.

VFX: Leans back out the window.
SFX: Taps the door of the car to move them along.

Officer: Well OK. Just get yourselves home as soon as you can... but take your time. Temperatures going to drop, and it will be like a skating rink in a couple of hours.

Tucker: Thanks Officer... don't worry. We'll be home-free long before then.

SFX: Car Accelerates past the officer and accident scene.
SFX: Car window rolls up

Where do you live?

Arnold: Really... just drop me anywhere. OK?

Tucker: You're really gonna piss me off, if you make me repeat every little question.

Arnold: Ah... Sumner St.

Tucker: What's the name of your favourite childhood pet?

Arnold: What?.... OK... OK.... ah... Dusty.

Tucker: Dusty Sumner... I can see it.

Arnold: I don't... I mean... I don't understand.

Tucker: It's simple. You put your favourite pet's name with the street where you live, and you get your porn star name.

Arnold: Porn star name?

Tucker: Yeah... you know... the name you'd go by if you were in a flesh flick.

Arnold: Oh.

Tucker: Guess mine...

Arnold: Um... Rov... errr.....?

Tucker: Not even close. Groovy Main.

Arnold: You had a dog named Groovy?

Tucker: Cat... Russian blue. Cute little thing. Course that was my old address. Sounds better than Groovy Cell Block F, dontcha think?

Arnold: You're kidding about the... uh... whole Tucker Macklin thing right?

Tucker: What's your name?

Arnold: Arnold.

Tucker: *(Harsh laugh)* Just Arnold. Who the hell are you... Madonna? Sting? Prince? You just get one name. Arnold? What is it your first or your last name?

Arnold: Beck. My last... my... my name is Arnold Beck.

Tucker: There you go... that wasn't so hard was it, Arnold Beck? Let me guess... you're a computer geek right, Arnold Beck?

Arnold: No... well... I use computers... but...

Tucker: Let me guess! I'm good at this shit. OK... um... you work for the government somewhere.. Bureaucrat or something. Work in a cubicle, right?

Arnold: No... I-

Tucker: Accountant! You're an accountant!

Arnold: Well... actually... more of a bookkeeper.

Tucker: Told ya, I'm good at this stuff.

Arnold: What's your name?

Tucker: You know my name.

Arnold: No... no...

Tucker: You know my name, Arnold. You got it in the first try. I mean. You oughta be happy. You're REAL smart, aren't you?

Arnold: No. Look, I won't tell anybody anything.

Tucker: Damned straight you won't! I don't know Arnie. I mean, on one hand I like you... but...

Arnold: I just want to go home. I don't want to do this.

Tucker: Hey, you stood out there... bold as brass... like you were some kinda knight or something. What the hell did you call it?

Arnold: What?

Tucker: You know... Rom. He was on a... case... or a crusade...

Arnold: Quest... a <u>noble</u> quest.

Tucker: Yeah...

Arnold: Look... you said it yourself. I'm nobody. We can just forget this whole thing. You know....
(Thinking of avoidance) There's a game I like to play...when I'm driving.

Tucker: Arnold.

Arnold: PLEASE! I know you'll like this one! It's like your Porn Star name game, but it's a twist.

Tucker: OK Arnold Beck, how do you play?

Arnold: Well, you have two people with names, the last names make a third person's name.

Tucker: I don't get it.

Arnold: I'll go first. It's fun... really! I just... I'm not good at explaining things.

Tucker: This is gettin' real boring <u>real </u>fast, Arnold.

Arnold: No, I'll give you the classic example. You'll like this one. It's from Bewitched. Remember that show?

Tucker: I thought you said you don't watch TV.

Arnold: I said I don't OWN a television. But I've seen some TV shows. Who hasn't seen Bewitched, right?

Tucker: OK... fine.

Arnold: OK... like a said, this is a classic. Dick Sergeant. Dick York... and you put their last names together and you get Sergeant York.

Tucker: *(Thinking)* Yeah... OK. I see that.

Arnold: Now, you go.

(Pause)
Tucker: I can't think of any.

Arnold: OK... OK... I'll go again.. Alright?

Tucker: Sure.

Arnold: Ah... Larry King... and uh.. Larry David... makes King David.

Tucker: I don't get it.

Arnold: Oh, come on. Sure you do... their last names... their first names are Larry...?

Tucker: Are you calling me stupid?

Arnold: No! NO... of course not.

Tucker: OK. I've got one...

Arnold: See... I told you you'd get the hang of it.

Tucker: The Larry King thing... gave me the idea.

Arnold: OK, go ahead.

Tucker: BB King...

Arnold: Yeah?

Tucker: Bea Arthur...

Arnold: uh-huh?

Tucker: Give you King Arthur... right?

Arnold: Well...

Tucker: RIGHT?

Arnold: Well, yeah... of course! I mean... you said BB King... and there's only one Bea for Bea Arthur... but still...

SFX: *Truck brakes are hit and it decelerates to a stop*
SFX: *Automatic gear thrown into park.*
Tucker: Maybe we should just end the ride right here.

Arnold: No! I mean... we're not in Truro.
(Silence.)

SFX: *Gear placed into "Drive" and the Truck begins accelerating again.*
Tucker: Sure... good point Arnold. I mean... No point in not taking you home. After all, I'd <u>love</u> to meet your wife. She must be REAL worried about you, right?

Scene 5: Benediction

Arnold: *(Distantly)* So tell me the truth... you're not really Macklin, right?

Tucker: You know the answer to that, Arnold.

Arnold: You're just playing with me. You're just trying to upset me. You almost had me going. I mean... you <u>can't</u> be Macklin...

Tucker: I'll bite... why am I <u>not</u> Macklin, Arnold?

Arnold: 'Cause you'd have to be pretty smart to get all the way from Ontario to here in just a couple of days. Avoid the whole manhunt.

Tucker: So, I'm not smart, huh?

Arnold: No! I told you I'm not good at explaining things. Look, I just mean... it's quite a coincidence.

Tucker: Maybe its fate, Arnold. You keep up on the news do you, Arnold?

Arnold: I told you I read. I read the paper every day. And well, I'm just saying... criminals always get caught somewhere. It's impressive that you made it this far.

Tucker: Maybe I'm no criminal.

Arnold: That's what I mean. Macklin wasn't a murderer. He was just somebody who robbed a bank once.

Tucker: Would have got away with it... they just nabbed one of my partners and...

Arnold: You're <u>not</u> Tucker Macklin.

Tucker: Stop. Friggin'. Saying. That.

Arnold: I'm sorry. I mean... you can't be. It's just... I'm sorry, I said I'd stop.

Tucker: Then shut you're goddamned mouth.

Arnold: It was only supposed to be Mary... She's the only one who knew.

Tucker: Knew what? What the hell are you talkin' about Arnold?

Arnold: You're right you know. Marriage is about making choices. Mary hates that I'm a bookkeeper. She's never said it straight out. But I know. I mean. It's in her eyes, every time I come home. We can't all be a noble quest, Mr. Macklin. At least... not until we've suffered. It's like being angry without a focus. I completely understand why you like Rom.

Tucker: What do ya mean?

Arnold: How you lose a little bit of your humanity to put on the righteous armor of the knight... But tell me... really. I won't tell. I'll keep quiet. I know how to keep a secret. You can be sure of that. You're not Macklin.

Tucker: Geezus. You're an idiot. You're a freakin' idiot, Arnold! Do I have to show you my club card. Look in the back of the cab!

Arnold: Yeah?

Tucker: What do you see?

Arnold: Some clothes...

Tucker: Turn on the light.

SFX: *Internal truck light turned on.*

Arnold: It's a... jump suit.. with a number on the front.

Tucker: These clothes I'm wearing were in the truck when I took it.. Lucky huh?

Arnold: And that's prisoner's garb in the back.

Tucker: *(Sarcastic)* You catch on <u>real</u> quick, Arnie.

Arnold: What happened to the people you stole the truck from?

Tucker: *(Trying to sound threatening)* You don't want to know now, do you really Arnold?

Arnold: *(Unfazed)* Actually I do Tucker.

Tucker: So at least you believe me now.

Arnold: Yeah I believe you. I know a little about your escape Tucker. They say you've been in and out of prison since you were a kid.

Tucker: Yeah, so what?

Arnold: Nothing... except... you're no murderer. You've never even assaulted anyone.

Tucker: Don't mean there's not a first time... Arnold. I -

Arnold: Don't worry Tucker... I won't tell. I told you that. I always keep my word. You don't have to threaten me. You know the thing about anger.

Tucker: Yeah? What about it??

Arnold: Nothing... I just find all this... well... rather... ironic.

Tucker: Yeah, why?

Arnold: The news reports all talk about a connection between your escape and the highway murders.

Tucker: I don't know nothin' about that.

Arnold: No, of course not, Tucker. You don't have a family, do you Tucker?

Tucker: What's that got to do with anything?

Arnold: Just making conversation... You wanted to meet my wife... I just remembered that the article said you had no family... juvenile hall to foster home... all your life, right?

Tucker: Yeah, so what?

Arnold: I never had kids. Not with the experiences of my father, but you really should consider marriage, Tucker. Yeah, it can be difficult... sure... But it's also... motivating.

Tucker: Turn off the light will ya?

Arnold: See... that's what my father taught me best, and I never got it until just a couple of weeks ago.

Tucker: I told you to turn off that light! It's hard enough to see driving the road in the storm without that light-

Arnold: I mean it just hit me. And then it all came together.

Tucker: What the hell are you talking about?

Arnold: The constant disappointment. You never really attain what you can become without cutting out the distractions.

Tucker: Distractions? What are you talking about?

Arnold: And you don't cut out the distractions until your anger reaches a critical mass.

Tucker: What the- ?

Arnold: And when it reaches threshold... when you can't think anymore. Like you're gonna scream. Poof. Just like that. Clarity. It's all so very clear.

Tucker: What the hell are you doing with that bag?

Arnold: I'm sorry Tucker. I told you I'm terrible at explaining things. Here, Look at this. You'll really want to see this.

SFX: Opening the doctor's bag.
Tucker: What the hell are you doing ... !? Take your hands outta the bag or I'll break 'em off!

Arnold: Just opening it for you to see Tucker. Then you'll know what I mean. Just look here... in my case.

SFX: Squealing on the brakes the truck slides into the snow bank..
Tucker: What? WHAT THE FU- WHAT IS THAT?!!?

Arnold: You wanted to meet my wife.

SFX: Struggling to open the driver's side door. Snow bank is making it difficult.
Tucker: That's a HEAD... Geezus Christ! That's a woman's head!!

Arnold: Rid the world of wickedness. I used to get so angry with Mary. It nearly drove me mad. She called it mid-life crisis. But it's not when it happens, it's who you are when it hits you. And then <u>clarity</u>. I told you. Mary was the first one to know. She can keep a secret now... so can you... Tucker.

SFX: *Banging on the car door with all his might. It starts to open. The wind howls.*
Tucker: HELP! Help! He's going to kill me!!!

Arnold: It's a noble quest, Tucker.

Tucker: God! Open... Dammit.. OPEN!!

SFX: *Door squeals open in the snow. Tucker staggers in the drifts.*

Arnold: Rom destroyed the shapeshifters Tucker. That's what they all are. There was this sweet girl I picked up first.... but she was a prostitute. That punk graffiti writer. He was top of his class. No one knew his shadowself.

VFX: *Screaming in the distance nearly swallowed up by the wind.*
Tucker: HELP! HELP!

Arnold: And... oh... the hitchhiker... You wouldn't believe the things <u>he</u> told me, Tucker.
Well, you have to start somewhere, right? I just hate living a lie too. Showing one face and having another. It. Makes. Me. So. ANGRY.
But it's so cleansing afterwards... like... I'm finally worthy. I wish Father could see me now.
He'd be so proud.

SFX: *Slide over to the driver's side.*
VFX: *Shouting outside the door.*

Where are you going Tucker? No one can hear you.

VFX: *Speaking back inside the cab.*
I know Mary. I know Mary... I KNOW MARY... I won't forget the knife.

SFX: *Fiddling in the bag pulls out a knife.*
Thank you dear.... No... I can do up my own top button. I know its cold out. Be back in a moment, OK? Just stay here where it's warm.

SFX: *Slams the door of the truck, but it doesn't shut completely. Too much snow stuck. The wind howls.*

(Long Pause)
VFX: *Tucker screams barely audible against the howling of the wind.*

(Long Pause)

SFX: *Single set of footsteps walking back to the car barely audible against the background of the wind.*
SFX: *Door of the truck squeaks open. Arnold enters. Rubs his hands together, and slams the door shut.*
VFX: *Arnold is whistling the chorus of the Big Rock Candy Mountain*
Well that was unpleasant, wasn't it?
I know... we'll have to ditch the truck. But we'll have some time before they identify the body.
No... its okay Mary... we'll find a place for Tucker. You know I wouldn't squeeze the two of you together like that. He'll just have to be comfortable on the seat beside you. Like my Grandmother used to say, if you don't behave, I'll give you your head and your hands to play with.
I really like that song. How did it go again Tucker?

SFX: *Drops the gears into "Drive" and they spin for a bit while the truck peals away on the slick road.*

VFX: *Arnold sings the chorus fading out to silence as Epilogue cuts in.*
(Singing)
In the Big Rock Candy Mountain, It's a land that's fair and bright,
The handouts grow on bushes, And you sleep out every night.
The boxcars all are empty, And the sun shines every day
I'm bound to go, Where there ain't no snow
Where the sleet don't fall, And the winds don't blow
In the Big Rock Candy Mountain....

Go ahead, join in Mary... oh right. *(Laughing)*... You're not very good at singing... You haven't got the lungs for it. *(More laughter)*
(Singing)
Oh the buzzin' of the bees, In the cigarette trees,
Near the soda water fountain, At the lemonade springs
Where the bluebird sings, On the big rock candy mountain.

Epilogue:
When someone claims to know the truth. Where clarity exists in the eyes of another, and their righteous hand sweeps in to shake yours, run screaming. For when a burning anger meets the long and weary road, beware of the hitchhiker... along the highways of the Shadowlands.

Greed: Ghosts of the Present

Prologue:
There is a Land that's somewhere beyond the horizon. You may catch a glimpse of it- when the sun sets, or in the moments before dawn. It's the twilight that flickers at the edge of imagination; somewhere between reality and fantasy. It's the place where monsters roam, and portals to other worlds wait in the back of a closet and in the crevices of your mind.
Welcome, to the Shadowlands....

As our scientific understanding increases we reach ever outwards trying to find the next plateau. But one of the unbending rules of life is that the more you know the more you need to learn. This lesson will become apparent to the crew of the Albion as they enter... the Shadowlands.

Act I: Set Sail
Scene 1: Bridge of the Albion

The Albion is a 50 year old ship that has been sold to Jarod Wilson. He is the third owner of the cargo hauler. The ship is round and uses its rotation through space to produce artificial gravity. The main method of sub-light propulsion is an artificial singularity projection drive (called the "Carrot drive." This refers to the carrot drawing the donkey forward). It pulls the ship forward evenly reducing stress on the hull rather than pushing the vessel through space.

The bridge of the ship is relatively quiet. Forward is a position for the navigator helmsman, the captain and a jump seat.

While not spacious, the bridge is not cramped either. There are constant read-outs depicting the status of the ship. The captain's seat is positioned centrally. Jarod sits in the captains chair. 1st mate Nan is at the helm and Tanya sits at navigation.

VFX: *Albion is the Ship's computer and speaks gently through local speakers all the time.*
SFX: *Controls and buttons flicking from navigation console.*

Tanya: We're clearing the sol system now... still within Pluto's orbit but far enough away that gravitation shouldn't interfere with the fold.

Jarod: Good. Do one last scan. I don't want any rogue asteroids or dark matter throwing the fold off course like the Danrakos delivery.

Tanya: *(Teasing)* You don't trust my intuition?

Jarod: *(Sarcastic)* I'd know better than to second guess a class "A" navigator on a class "D" freighter. However, all the psychic energy in the known universe don't fill our pockets.

Nan: Might make you think they're full though.

Jarod: If we don't have enough money to replace the singularity projector in the next ten folds we won't be making any more deliveries. And that makes getting paid a challenge.

Tanya: Pay? That would be an interesting switch.

Jarod: Jarod's rule of merchant high finance of the stars... when you can't afford a Corporate navigator, find one to marry.

Nan: Ooh.. That's cold skip.

Tanya: That's OK Nan, give him his moment. He spent all day thinking on that zinger. He'll spend all night outside the cabin rethinking why he didn't clean scrub vents instead.

Nan: Krath! Could you two please save your lovers quarrel for later? Unless you hadn't noticed, we're on the clock and that bonus is shriveling each moment we delay.

Jarod: Quite right.

Nan: Scan's packed.

SFX: *Controls and buttons flicking from computer*

Forwarding the new info to your console, Tanya.

Tanya: Thanks.

Jarod: Albion.

VFX: *Albion speaks all lines with an ethereal voice*
Albion: Yes, Captain?

Jarod: Begin calculations for spatial fold; factor in the new information from navigation.

Albion: Of course Captain. I am a Generation-8 AI. I don't calculate mistakes, through omission or otherwise.

Jarod: Everybody's got a funny bone, it seems.

Albion: I need no bones Captain. I am not an everybody. I am an everything.

Nan: *(Points to the ceiling mumbling frustrated)* 'God' there, is so fettin' smug.. I wish I could throttle its personality down some.

Albion: Prejudice toward non-organics not withstanding-

Nan: - Maybe just its sense of superiority-

Albion: I require data from the fold drives.

VFX: *Slight modulation speaking through microphone*
Jarod: *(Into a microphone)* Bridge to Drive Room.

VFX/SFX: *Engineering beeps and is distant.*
Scott: *(Far away and faint)* WHAT NOW!
    (Closer) Ya, skip?

Jarod: Albion is waiting on the readout for the fold drives. What's the hold up?

Scott: The electron accelerators for drive two and three need calibrating.

Jarod: Can we jump without it?

Scott: *(Long pause, patronizing tone)* Yeaaaaah.. but I wouldn't recommend it.

Jarod: I recall hearing that before.

Tanya: *(To herself)* Deja vu is very comforting.

Scott: Good, then we can all sing it from rote together. "If we don't calibrate the electron accelerators before we jump, we run a high chance of a miss-fold." With my luck possibly to a place were we wont be able to get a star fix, or to the doorstep of my last girlfriend's apartment cubex. And then where would we be?

Jarod: What was her name again?

Scott: *(Shudders)* I'll tell ya where, some place you don't know where you are... and this time without tequila to blame.

Jarod: *(Long sigh)* How long?

Scott: Half a day.

Nan: Krath!

Jarod: Hear that? Nan's diplomatic tongue speaks for me too. You have got an hour and a half... Do what you can. Get Toby if you need help.

Scott: Get Toby's help? That's how I woke up in her apartment last time. I'll be lucky to get one drive aligned in less than two hours, Skip. I just can't-

Jarod: Scott! You're wasting time. One out of alignment is better than two- get to work!

SFX: *Snaps off communication.*

(Ends conversation with the Drive Room, rubs his face with frustration) It's like having children.

Nan: We're still in the room, Skip. Aren't you supposed to say stuff like that behind out backs?
(Unlatches herself out of the helm control.)
I'm going down to the Drive Room and see if I can prod Scott along.

SFX: *Door slides open and shuts.*

Tanya: You know, they're not a military crew.

Jarod: Makes no difference. I'm the Captain of this tub. Since when are orders up for conversation, military or merchant?

Tanya: Look, I'm Corporate. I'm used to taking orders. Scott grew up on the Spindle working as a tier tech. Nan's a 3rd gen cargo hauler. If I recall, you left the military 'cause you didn't like the way they did things.

Jarod: I just don't appreciate hypocrisy.

Tanya: Point is, everyone here is most likely civilian and NOT military for the same reason.

SCENE 2: Drive Room
The low hum of machinery in the background. Scott is working. A door slides open and Nan enters, Scott is singing to himself.

SFX: *Drive Room sound effects. Banging. Clank and whirring of tools*
VFX: *Scott whistle the tune "Whistle while you work" a little off-key*

Scott: *(Singing)* Whistle while you die, We fold and then we'll fry, so listen to my, listen to my, lis-

Nan: It is a good thing you're a tech, you'd get mighty hungry falling back on your singing career.

Scott: Hey Nan, didn't smell you there. So, Skip's a little testy huh?

Nan: Yeah, we're children.

SFX: *Pitches a part down the hall.*
Scott: Skip's kids huh? And you think my singing is bad. Imagine his kids.

Nan: Might be faster with the drives though.

Scott: You here to help or get in the way?

Nan: I'll help. What can I do, Scotty?

Scott: DON'T call me Scotty

Nan: Oh? I think it's cute.

Scott: Just because I have the same name and occupation as a fictional character from a 450 year old broadcast--

Nan: -Fine... no Scotty. No need to burn critical about it. What needs doing?

Scott: Check the particle flow density on the matter separator?

Nan: The 'what' on the 'where?'

Scott: *(Slowly)* Go down there and read the numbers off the screen to me. Tell me if they go over point 655.

SFX: *Nan walks away. Door slides open as Toby enters.*

Toby: All the cargo is squared away. How come we ain't folded?

Scott: Not now, I'm busy.

VFX: *From the distance.*
Nan: It says point 663

Scott: *(Mutters a curse)* Flarch. Albion!

Albion: Yes Engineer Montgomery.

Scott: Restrict the particle flow density on the matter separator by point zero one.

Albion: Restricting flow.

Toby: Hey is this supposed to---

Scott: -Toby, I swear to whatever god still answers prayers, if you touch anything, I will space everything you own.

Nan: It says point 632 now.

Scott: Cockroach invested Rojack.

SFX: *Kicking a bulkhead.*

Nan: Point 652

VFX: Make face kiss sound.
Scott: MMMuwha... I love you

Scene 3: Bridge
Sometime later.

VFX: *Voices fade in.*
Jarod: And that is why I don't think that we should have kids yet... whatdaya think?

(Long pause)

Albion: I believe your premise lacks conviction. You are focusing on logical means to enforce your point. Humans are not logical creatures... *(adding diplomatically)* in such circumstances. I do not understand your hesitation toward procreation. It is human nature to survive at any cost, and procreation is part of survival, thus the basis of your programming. Therefore you are defying-- Navigator Wilson will enter the bridge in 4 seconds Captain Wilson.

Jarod: OK. We'll save this for another time.

SFX: *Door sliding open and closing*
Albion: Of course, Captain Wilson.

Tanya: Of course what?

Jarod: Nothing. How close can you get to the drop-off point when we jump? Deadline's here.

Tanya: I think we could recover an hour or so, but we'll be really close to the system.

Jarod: I trust ya.

VFX: *Into mic*
Scott... times up.

Scott: It's as good as it's gonna get; without more time there's nothing more I can do.

Jarod: There's never enough time Scott.. my advice is- 'get used to it.' Albion. Begin the calculations for spatial fold. Gather information from the Drive Room.

Albion: Beginning fold calculations.

MUSIC: *Exciting building music*
SFX*: Snaps on microphone*
VFX*: Through microphone, echoing on ship's comm speakers in bridge*
Jarod: Attention all hands. We are beginning fold calculations. Everyone to their seats. Nan, I need you at helm. Scott, last check on the singularity projector?

Scott: On it, Skip.

SFX: *Door sliding open and closing.*

Nan: Alright. Let's sail this boat.

SFX*: Nan puts on harness.*

Nan: Ceasing rotation. Shutting down internal gyro.

Albion: Calculations at 13%.

VFX*: Toby through speaker.*
Toby: Cargo is battened down and good to go in the hold, Skip. Ship shape and bristol fashion. I am locking myself in.

VFX*: Scott through speaker.*
Scott: All's "green" with the singularity projector, Skip.

Albion: Calculations at 20%.

Tanya: Navigational metrics unchanged.

Nan: Gyro is *off-line*, firing counter rotation jets... Zero-G in ten... *(starts counting down to one)*

VFX: *Scott through speaker.*
Scott: Particle stream up... optimum efficiency.. *(Under his breath)* Damn I'm good.

Albion: Calculations at 35%.

VFX: *Scott through speaker.*
Scott: Singularity projector on-line, charged in ten seconds. *(Counts down to one)*

Nan: We have zero gravity.

Tanya: Albion. Sensors read a fluctuation of point 5 g's. Adjusting navigational metrics.

Albion: Confirmed. Calculations at 44%.

Jarod: Will that effect the fold calculation, Albion?

VFX: *Scott through speaker.*
Scott: Singularity Projector charged.

Albion: Check sum... I can compensate for the change in metrics. Calculations at 50%.

Jarod: Good. Fire the Singularity Projector.

VFX: *Scott through speaker.*
Scott: Put your head between your legs and kiss your ass good-bye, Singularity Projector is go.

Nan: Confirmed. Singularity Projector is a go.

SFX: *The ship shudders and jerks forward.*

Tanya: We *have* a rift. Probing now.

Nan: The rift has us and we're moving. 50 KPS. *(starts counting up in increments of 25 to 150 kps)*

Albion: Calculations at 59%.

Tanya: Rift is good. We are on target.

VFX*: Scott through speaker.*
Scott: Stabilizing singularity.

Nan: Approaching Paw-nar.

SFX*: Claxons trigger in alarm.*

Nan: *(Frustrated)* Flarch! It's the PONR alert.

Tanya: Gets me every time.

Albion: Calculations at 78%.

SFX*: Claxons stop.*

Jarod: Scott, I thought we disengaged the Point of No Return alert 5 months ago?

VFX*: Scott through speaker.*
Scott: I've had my hands busy with the Drives. Besides I fix things. You want something broken talk to Toby.

VFX*: Scott through speaker.*
Toby: Hey! What did I do?

Nan: We are on course and past paw-nar.

Albion: Calculations at 97%.

Tanya: Entering the rift in ten. *(Counts down to one)*

Albion: Calculations at 100% establishing hull harmonics.

Nan: We're now entering the rift.

Jarod: I hate this part.

(Silence)

MUSIC: *Exciting transitional music*

ACT II: Everywhere
Scene 1: Bridge of Albion

VFX: Fade in..
Nan: So I'll be the first to ask the obvious question. Where the hell are we?

SFX: Snapping controls.
Jarod: Not where we're supposed to be. That's for damn sure. Tanya?

Tanya: We should be at Alpha Centauri.

Jarod: Great. Just once I'd like something to happen around here. It's always so gosh-fettin' boring.

Nan: There goes our bonus.

Tanya: Ummm... *(Concerned pause)* Where are all the stars?

Jarod: Albion? Where are we?

Nan: *(Just noticing the starless void herself)* Where the flarch ARE all the stars?

Albion: Alpha Centauri.

Jarod: No we're not.

Albion: Nevertheless, all sensors, metrics and calculations verify that we are at Alpha Centauri.

Jarod: *(Slow breath in and out)* OK. Let's figure this out. Nan, let's have gravity.

Nan: *(A little stunned but snapping back into action)* Right..... right Skip. Starting gyro... Firing rotation jets.

SFX: *Jets firing and begin Albion rotation for gravity.*

VFX: *Scott through speaker.*
Scott: Drive Room here. What did you do?

Jarod: What?

VFX: *Scott through speaker.*
Scott: What in Tegret's name did you do up there? Gravity's off the scale! But I can't get a constant! It's fluctuating more'n my stomach on Toby's lasagna night. You decide to jump through a black hole!?!

Jarod: Interesting theory, Albion?

Albion: Unlikely.

Nan: Why?

Albion: You are still alive.

VFX: *Scott through speaker.*
Scott: Well, I want to know what the flarch is going on NOW. How am I supposed to fix any-

Jarod: -Not now Scott.

SFX: *Shuts off speaker.*

Nan?

Nan: Yes?

Jarod: What did we do?

Nan: Still trying to figure that out, Skip. We've got spin. Deck gravity is good.

Jarod: Unharness and give me an assessment. Now.

SFX: *Sounds of buckles and clasps opening.*

Tanya: I don't like this.

Jarod: Is that your official assessment?

Tanya: Just.. just a feeling...

Jarod: As ship's psychic.. I'll log that as a 'Yes'. Albion, where are we?

Albion: Alpha Centau-

Jarod: -Belay that! I may not be a Mark XIV, Model 362A-

Albion: -362*B*.

Jarod: *(Pauses)* Look. We're in the midst of a dark nebula or something. There's no sign of the stars. Forget the established coordinates; give me some raw sensor data of what's directly outside our hull!

SFX: *Sounds of Albion's sensor grid processing information.*
Albion: That's interesting.

Nan: I'm not getting any stellar or planetary bodies on scopes.

Albion: I'm not registering Alpha Centauri on deep or shallow scan.

Jarod: Now we're getting somewhere. *(Pause with a soft bitter laugh.)* Getting somewhere in nowhere. Where's that lead us?

Albion: However, that is not what I find interesting, Captain Wilson.

SFX: *Doors struggle open and Toby enters*

Toby: Is there anything I can-

Jarod: *(Frustrated)* Stow it Toby- What's interesting, Albion?

Albion: We are not alone as Officer Barlow suggests.

Jarod: What?

Albion: Refocusing starboard dorsal cameras to C level magnification now.

Nan: What the hell...? That's a ship!

Jarod: Not a ship of the line. I know all the schematics of vessels out this far. That hull's not-

Toby: -Flarch!.. That's the Remus!

SFX: *Leaning forward and clicking buttons*
Jarod: What?.. No.. The Remus has been gone for 100-

Toby: -107...

Jarod: And it's sure as Tegret's armpit not gonna be here in the middle of-

Tanya: -Nowhere.

Toby: *(Softly but gleefully)* Krath. This is our lucky day.

Jarod: Nan... call up Scott. I'm not willing to take Toby's word alone on this. *(To Toby)* No offense.

Albion: Historical records of that era are not fully integrated into my system, however the vessel's hull tonnage and markings are identical to that of the Remus. There's no transmission coming from the ID beacon.

Jarod: Call up Scott.

Toby: But Skip, do you know how much salvage-

Jarod: - Let's drop this talk to idle... At least until Scott's here. We don't even entertain the thought that it's more than a sensor ghost till Montgomery gives us a report.

Toby: But Skip we can retire-

(Silence representing the palpable look from Jarod.)

...OK, Skip.

Jarod: I want everyone in the Mess in ten minutes. We gotta figure out where we are and how we get out.

Scene 2: Mess Hall
The mess hall is a narrow room, with metal shelving and a long metal bar-like countertop on one side. The other side has tables and benches that swing down from the opposite wall, and a series of folding chairs secured against the end. Freeze dried food dispensers, microwave heating unit, and an old fashion tin pot for coffee and tea are available. All cutlery and dishware are metal.

SFX: *A group of people enter the Mess and draw chairs and benches around a table.*

Jarod: This is what we know so far: Nothing. We've got no real information from metrics, sensors, or star coordinates.

(Long pause)

Scott: Is this the part where I say, "I told you so?"

Nan: Krath Scott! That doesn't help.

Jarod: Quiet! I want to know where we are and how we get out.

Toby: But-

Tanya: -Physically, psychically, even metaphorically--- We're nowhere.

Toby: ... the Remus-

Jarod: -Not good enough.

Albion: I have reviewed all ship records available since first logged space travel. There is no mention of such a phenomena.

Nan: Perfect.

Toby: Hello? has anyone else noticed the huge colony ship floating right there, asking to be towed to the nearest spaceport, making us all rich, famous, and thusly highly attractive to women, right Nan?

(Another pause.)

Nan: So, now what?

Scott: Here's the good news, the electron accelerators are fused and I can't fix them. They need to be replaced.

Jarod: How is that good news?

Scott: Because compared to the fact that I have nothing to replace them with its fettin' peachy.

Toby: No problem! The Remus only has about a *billion* injectors and enough replacement parts for thirty jumps. If only we knew someone around here who could take advantage of this valuable salvage!

Jarod: Will that work?

Scott: The Singularity Projector concept has not really changed in the last 100 years. There's different designs, but even if it's wildly different, I could still adapt it... *(Lower and under breath)* probably.

Jarod: Good, Tanya? Albion? Back to where we are?

Tanya: I... I don't know... it is like I've been cut off from the universe.

Albion: Captain Wilson, I have a working theory.

Jarod: OK Albion, I'm listening.

Albion: Since we have been here. I have not needed to adjust for stellar drift.

Jarod: So?

Tanya: That's not possible.

Jarod: Why?

Albion: Everything in space has stellar drift. It is part of the universe dragging matter as it expands. I accommodate for stellar drift autonomically, so I am embarrassed to report, the lack of drift went unnoticed initially.

Jarod: So there's no stellar drift?

Albion: Correct.

Nan: That still doesn't answer where we are.

Albion: But it does tell us where we are not. We must therefore be... outside.

Toby: Outside? Outside of what.

Albion: Outside of the universe.

(Stunned silence)

Tanya: That would explain why I don't know where we are. Theoretically, I should be able to determine position anywhere in the universe, but I'm blind.

Jarod: *(Pause)* We're going to have to hook up with the Remus then. Toby suit up. You know that ship. At a hundred and seven years, we're not going to get an easy corridor. You're going to have to make us a custom dock. So get out there and give us a link.

Toby: Sure thing, Skip.

Jarod: Now everybody. Let's not bog down on thinking about being outside the universe. Better to leave that flarch for poets, shrinks, physicists, and other dunsels. We've got a problem. We need a solution. Stations.

VFX: Series of "Aye, sirs" and "Skips" from all assembled.
SFX: Moving chairs as everyone heads back to work.
MUSIC: Transitional growing suspense.

Scene 3: Spacewalk
Toby is floating in space, using maneuvering thrusters fastened on a belt pack. Scott is monitoring him from the bay area, keeping a tight visual through the large view glass. As we enter the scene, Toby is halfway across. The scene cuts back and forth inside and outside of Albion.

SFX: Sounds of maneuvering thrusters firing. Stopping, and re-firing in short bursts throughout Toby's "walk" in space.
    Sounds of a monitoring station working as Scott keeps an eye out for dangers.

VFX: *Toby speaking through his helmet.*
SFX: *Respirator breathing. Slight thruster motion.*
Toby: Is it me, or is it quiet?

VFX: *Scott through Toby's helmet speaker.*
Scott: It's called space, moron. It tends to know how to hold an echo.

VFX: *Toby speaking through his helmet.*
SFX: *Respirator breathing. Slight thruster motion.*
Toby: Even space tends to give a background RF sound.

VFX: *Scott through Toby's helmet speaker.*
Scott: Well, if Tanya's right...there's no radio frequencies to be heard.

SFX: *Respirator breathing. More thruster motion.*
VFX: *Toby speaking through his helmet.*
Toby: She freaks me out.

VFX: *Scott through Toby's helmet speaker.*
Scott: Who?

VFX: *Toby speaking through his helmet.*

SFX: *Respirator breathing. Slight thruster motion.*
Toby: Tanya. Psychics. The whole fettin' group of them. I don't trust 'em.

VFX: *Scott through Toby's helmet speaker.*
Scott: I wouldn't worry about it. Skip's not.

VFX: *Toby speaking through his helmet.*
SFX: *Respirator breathing. Slight thruster motion.*
Toby: I don't get the attraction. I wouldn't want any woman readin' my mind.

VFX: *Scott through Toby's helmet speaker.*
Scott: I'm sure if Tanya tried, she'd come away with a real vacant whistle in her ears.

VFX: *Toby speaking through his helmet.*
SFX: *Respirator breathing. Slight thruster motion.*
Toby: Yeah.. yeah... very funny. I'm coming around the starboard baffle plate now.

VFX: *Scott through Toby's helmet speaker.*
Scott: There should be an airlock just on the dorsal side. It's where they bring up the cargo. Should be a good size portal.

VFX: *Jarod's voice breaks in through Toby's helmet speaker..*
Jarod: And I wouldn't worry about me, Toby. I didn't exactly marry Tanya for her mind anyway.

VFX: *Toby speaking through his helmet.*
SFX: *Respirator breathing. Slight thruster motion.*
Toby: Skip?! I.. I didn't mean-

SFX: *Perspective changes to inside Albion. Jarod and Scott talking in a small room with readouts flashing and blinking. Toby's voice over the speaker.*
   Jarod flips the "Send" button before speaking.

Jarod: I'll make you a deal Toby. You get this hookup done without incident, and I won't tell my wife that she freaks you out.

VFX: *Toby's voice through speaker.*
SFX: *Slight thruster and breathing of respirator sounds through speaker.*
Toby: *(Pause)* And I'll keep to myself that you said you didn't marry her for her mind.

SFX: *Snap on "Send" button.*

Jarod: Actually, you'll keep that to yourself, or I'll kill you.

VFX: *Toby's voice through speaker.*
SFX: *Slight thruster and breathing of respirator sounds through speaker.*
Toby: Or I'll just keep that to myself.

SFX: *Snaps off "Send" button. Scott and Jarod speak without Toby listening in.*
VFX: *Toby's voice is heard in the background.*

Jarod: How's he doing?

Scott: He's on target. All readings are OK. This is a walk in the park, Skip.

VFX: *Toby's voice distantly through speaker.*
Toby: So, a guy goes to the law office and he's sitting in front of the lawyer.

Jarod: *(Pause)* I don't much like the landscape, that's all. You keep an eye on him. When he gets a lock, we get the umbilical set up, get the pieces and find our way somewheres fast.

VFX: *Toby's voice distantly through speaker.*

Toby: "I made love with my wife." the guy says. "You made love to your wife?" The Lawyer asks? "Yeah," The guy says and I want a divorce."

Scott: You got it Skip.

Jarod: What's he doing now?

VFX: *Toby's voice distantly through speaker.*
Toby: "I don't understand," says the lawyer. "It's simple," the guy says. "After we were finished my wife told me I was a wonderful lover."

Scott: Jokes. He always tells jokes when he's nervous.

Jarod: I'll be on the Bridge. Let's get it done.

SFX: *Door opens and shuts behind him*

SFX: *Perspective changes. Back "outside" with Toby. Respirator breathing. Slight thruster motion.*
VFX: *Toby speaking through his helmet.*
Toby: "You want to divorce your wife because she tells you, you're a wonderful lover?" the Lawyer says baffled.
     "Oh no.." says the man, "I want to divorce her for knowing the difference!"

SFX: *Muted thud and clang as Toby touches down on the Remus. Noise reverberating in his helmet. Hand begins pulling himself along handrails.*

OK.. I've got contact. Finding connection ports for manual umbilical.

VFX: *Scott through Toby's helmet speaker.*
Scott: I think you're contagious Toby. I'm getting juiced. What's she like?

VFX: *Toby speaking through his helmet.*

SFX: *Grind as Toby manually turns wheels to open up entrance.*
Toby: Pure golden Scott. We should toe this baby back with us, and sell her whole. Get that planetoid I've been lookin' to retire on.

VFX: *Scott through Toby's helmet speaker.*
Scott: First things first.

VFX: *Toby speaking through his helmet.*
Toby: I've got the autolock disengaged on the Remus iris valve. Once we get the corridor set we should be able to remote open the doors without much trouble.

VFX: *Scott through Toby's helmet speaker.*
Scott: I can't see you from where I am, but I'm getting a little torque on the line.

VFX: *Toby speaking through his helmet.*
Toby: I've got the lines fastened secure. You can remote power them up and pull over the corridor. Just checkin' one more thing and I'll haul it back.

SFX: *Perspective changes to inside Albion. Scott talking to himself by docking control with readouts flashing and blinking. Toby's voice over the speaker.*
      Scott flips the "Send" button before speaking.
Scott: Alrighty.. Be careful, I'm still registering some drag.

VFX: *Toby's voice through speaker.*
Toby: *(Laughing softly)* What, you wanna live forever?

SFX: *Scott snaps off "Send" button.*
Scott: *(To himself)* We're not drifting I don't... Oh flarch!

SFX: *Scott snaps on intercom to Bridge.*
Bridge.. this is Scott. Kill our gravity!

VFX: *Jarod's voice over speaker.*
Jarod: What's the problem, Chief?

Scott: Toby's got the lines connected, but we're rotating and the Remus isn't. Without normal space drift-

VFX: *Jarod's voice over speaker.*
Jarod: -We're dragging the line. *(Turning from speaker)* All hands kill G-rotation now!

SFX: *Scott snaps on "Send" button to Toby.*
Scott: Toby!. Look alive! We're spinning a little fast to-- Tegrin's name! Look out for-

VFX: *Toby's voice through speaker.*
Toby: Oh.. Flar--

SFX: *A short burst of static cuts off Toby's transmission and then dead silence.*

Scott: Toby!

SFX: *Health monitors broadcasting from Toby's suit and registering on Scott's board go wild and then flatline.*

Scott: TOBY!

MUSIC: *Ominous Transitional*

Scene 4: Bridge
Jarod, Scott, Tanya, and Nan are all arguing bitterly.
MUSIC: *Transition*
VFX: *Fade in with everyone arguing overtop of each other.*

Jarod: Enough! Let's just keep to the facts.

Nan: The facts are Toby's in a body bag which is gonna get a lot more cramped if we don't get outta-

Jarod: -Scott! What did you find.

Scott: *(Distantly, almost despondent)* I went out after him. The cable pinned him down against the Remus. I'm not a doctor but, I don't think it was the pressure- least not from the umbilical link. His vacc suit had a couple tears in it. My guess is he rubbed against something sharp along the hull. It's fettin' stupid.

Tanya: *(Sympathetically)* You mustn't blame yourself.

Scott: Me? I told him to watch himself. When we spun into view, it's like he was standing there dumbfounded, staring at something.. the thing is....

Jarod: What?

Scott: I swear I saw something out there. Right where he was?

Jarod: What do you mean you saw something?

Scott: It was probably a trick from our floods. I don't know. It looked like someone else was out there.

Nan: Brilliant. All in favour of untethering ourselves from this death ship say "Aye!..."

SFX: *Raises her hand*
"Aye!"

Jarod: Let's calm down now. We're not going anywhere.

Scott: Did you forget about the electron accelerators? Without some replacements we might as well park here and try to garner some interest as a used transport lot.

Nan: Well you can grab those replacement parts, I'm sitting right-

Jarod: -Belay that! No one is staying on Albion. We'll need all hands to get what we need. Pack yourself some tools-

Nan: -But Skip I-

Jarod: *(Gently)* -Won't be nothing Nan. Besides, you're always saying I never give you time to sightsee. What could be better than taking a tour of no place on a legendary ship 100 years-

Scott: -107-

Jarod: -107 years lost.

Nan: *(Reluctantly)* OK...

Jarod: Good. Now go ahead and get us some packs together. We'll need the dolly and the winches. Be careful, without gravity, its going to be a fettin' mess to push that dolly through the corridor. Make certain we've got some wide lumination headlamps for the vacc suits. Can't tell if there's any juice left in the old girl.

Nan: *(Steeling herself)* OK.. OK, Skip.

SFX: *Door opens and Nan floats out the hatch leaving the Bridge. Door shuts.*

Jarod: Get back on the corridor. Make sure our bridge is solid and there's no more surprises. We want to make certain there's no more accidents.

Scott: Yeah.. sure. You know.. I was thinking. We could begin spinning again once I recheck the umbilical corridor. It shouldn't give any stress on the supports once we're moving, and we'll have gravity on Remus.

Jarod: That's a good thought, Albion?

Albion: Engineer Montgomery is correct Captain Wilson. With some care, I could vary our acceleration so that we have a minimum stress upon either the bridge we've erected, or the Remus. Struts are solidly linked into both hulls. The Remus would experience a lesser gravity, but it would be enough.

Jarod: Let's prepare for that option, but wait till we board and check the structure of the Remus. It may appear solid, but I don't want us tearing it to pieces.

Scott: I hate zero G... It's going to take me twice as long to pull myself to docking.

Jarod: On your way, Scott.

Scott: Aye, Skip.

SFX: *Door opens the door and Scott floats out the hatch leaving the Bridge. Door shuts.*

Jarod: You're strangely quiet.

Tanya: I'm feeling useless here. Can't navigate... and I'm not able to sense...

Jarod: Sense? Sense what?

Tanya: I never told you this before Honey... but .. I'm a precog.

Jarod: Precog? What?!

Tanya: It's not exactly something that people feel comfortable about. I mean, most people are freaked out enough about psychic's reading their minds-

Jarod: -Actually Toby-

Tanya: -I knew.

Jarod: You.. knew. I should have guessed that.

Tanya: That's the thing.. the precognition stuff.. its just flashes. Possibilities, options. Warnings to go right instead of left. We're taught in Esper Academy to keep that to yourself. Norms go nuts when they think you know something about the future. They need to know, and hate you for it if it's not exactly what they pictured.

Jarod: OK...

Tanya: .. That's why I didn't say anything. I didn't want to burden.

Jarod: That's the point of a marriage Tanya. If you can't burden me.. what's the fettin' point of complaining about marriage?

Tanya: You're upset.

Jarod: You read my mind.

Tanya: OK.. I can understand that.. but listen. I don't sense anything. No possibilities. I should have sensed that THIS was going to happen. It's pretty big, don't you think?... and I didn't get anything. Where ever we are, we're beyond real space.

Jarod: So you said-

Tanya: -We're beyond any normal state...even death.

Jarod: You'd better get suited up.

Tanya: Did you hear me, Jarod?

Jarod: You'd better get suited up.

MUSIC: Transitional

Scene 5: The Remus
All four of the Albion crew are suited up in vacc suits. Each holds a corner of the dolly and are pulling themselves down the "umbilical corridor" between Albion and Remus. The umbilical is a 10' across roughly hexagonal shape of durable but malleable polymer design. The polymer is able to hold a charge, so it remains eerily lit up as it completes the circuit between the two vessels.

VFX: *All the characters in this scene are speaking through their vacc suit helmets with the exception of Albion who reverberates through the helmet speakers.*
SFX: *As each character speaks in this scene, there's the background whisper of the respirator breathing. Albion is the only exception however, as Albion speaks, the character listening is still using his respirator.*

Jarod: Look alive people. Just forty more metres and we're there. Keep the dolly away from the umbilical's sides.

Scott: Albion...

Albion: Yes, Engineer Montgomery?

Scott: Have you begun rotation?

Albion: Yes, Engineer Montgomery. I have edged thrusters at point zero-zero seven. Is there a problem?

Scott: No.. I just wanted to make sure you began. I don't feel any change.

Albion: I calculate that at the current rate of acceleration, gravity should begin to manifest in 4 minutes and 36 seconds. I can exceed safety recommendations by a 17% margin, if you wish-

Jarod: - 4 minutes and 36 seconds will be just fine Albion. Let's not throw any more risk into this than we need.

Albion: As you wish Captain Wilson. 4 minutes 25 seconds remaining.

Scott: *(Mumbling to himself)* I hate zero-G.

Nan: I'd rather be pushing cargo at zero-G than muscling it through.

Jarod: Hold up... Scott, power up the outer doors.

Scott: On it Skip...

(Pause)
SFX: *Sound of a buttons being punched and a metallic hand crank moving.*
Ready.

Jarod: Train those lights on the interior. Albion's read no life onboard.. but I'm not about to take chances. Keep frosty. Clear?

Nan: Clear.

Scott: Aye, Skip.

Tanya: Understood.

Jarod: Crack it open Scott.

SFX: *Doors grind, whine, and slowly open. They halt after a half a foot.*
Ahh... Scott?

Scott: These circuits are pretty old Skip. *(Mumbles to the door)* Come on old girl.. open or I'll rewire your innards into a toaster!

SFX: *Doors whine and resume opening, echoing as they retract fully.*
See, you just gotta know how to talk to 'em... kinda like a woman.

Nan: Hence, why you're still single.

Albion: 2 minutes before binding gravity reaffirms, Crew.

Tanya: I thought the dolly was getting a little more difficult to move along the tracks.

Jarod: Thanks Albion. Keep monitoring all crew and Remus.
Let's move in. Get what we're looking for.

Scott: Toby was the one who knew the schematics of the Remus. But if we work towards the aft, we should be able to find conduits to thruster and drive assemblies.

Jarod: It's pitch black in there.. work in teams of two. Scott and Nan you're together, Tanya you're with me.

Tanya: I've never done a salvage-

Jarod: -operation, I know. That's why you're with me. I'm an old hand at this. Nan and Scott should work fast together. We're going to the bridge.

MUSIC: *Transitional*

ACT III: SPIRITS
Scene 1: Lights On

Tanya and Jarod enter the Bridge, a small chamber rigged to run everything to three consoles. All three chairs are unoccupied. Not even dust is caked on the machinery or seats. All power is out, and the only light source comes from the headlamps.

VFX: All the characters in this scene are speaking through their vacc suit helmets with the exception of Albion who reverberates through the helmet speakers.

SFX: As each character speaks in this scene, there's the background whisper of the respirator breathing. Albion is the only exception however, as Albion speaks, the character listening is still using his respirator.

SFX: The sound of a manual winch banging into the closed sliding doors. The winch pulls the doors apart about six inches. The huff and puff of Jarod and Tanya as they each pull the doors open.

Tanya: *(Catching her breath)* Well, that took longer than expected.

Jarod: Yeah, with the lifts out, and all the hatches sealed, its a grunt.

Tanya: Gonna be a chore moving the accelerators out at this rate.

Jarod: That's why we're here.

SFX: Begins manually snapping consoles. Power begins to hum from the station.
Looks like everything works at least- wait... hmm... that's not good.

Tanya: What is it?

Jarod: AI's gone.. Can't tell if it fragmented, or was wiped on purpose. Either way, there's no vestige of the regular AI. Scott?

SFX: *Scott speaks through their helmets.*
Scott: *(Puffing)* What?!

Jarod: I catch you before your nap?

SFX: *Scott speaks through their helmets.*
Scott: This fettin' pecktid dungoolen's giving us a little trouble coming out.

Jarod: You found something?

SFX: *Scott speaks through their helmets.*
Scott: Yup... and its unqualified good news for a change. The accelerators are in good condition and totally compatible with what we've got. Fact is.. they might even be rated for higher performance than the flarch-ridden poges we've been stuck with. I've got three accelerators, MORE'n enough.

Jarod: Great! Can Nan work on taking out the struts of the one giving you troubles there by herself for a bit?

SFX: *Nan speaks through their helmets.*
Nan: er, Captain?

SFX: *Scott speaks through their helmets.*
Scott: Umm.. sure, but she doesn't sound like she's really up for it, why?

Jarod: Bridge is in good condition. Looks like "Light's Out" shut everything down. But the AI is gone.

SFX: *Scott speaks through their helmets.*
Scott: Gone?

Jarod: Yeah...

SFX: *Scott speaks through their helmets.*
Scott: What do you mean gone?

Jarod: Don't know. You've got a portable comp back on Albion right?

SFX: *Scott speaks through their helmets.*
Scott: Yeah? Let me guess...

Jarod: Yeah. Congratulations, you're a mother.

SFX: *Scott speaks through their helmets.*
Scott: Alright...

Tanya: He's a... mother...?

Jarod: Well usually that's only the first part of a description for Scott. But in this case, he's about to give birth to a new AI.

Tanya: You're going to bring Albion over here?

Jarod: Just a copy. I can get the CO_2 scrubbers working on oxygen, but if we want to get full power up and running we're going to need an AI to be in control. Can you think of a better AI, available?

Tanya: *(Slight dizzying moan of pain)* nnnngg...

Jarod: *(Not paying attention)* OK, any other AI available?

Tanya: *(Screams as hot knives feel like they are tearing at her temples.)*

Scene 2: Ghosts in the Machine
Drive Shaft 27A is dark enough to be a mine shaft. Tracks lead down the floor way to aid in maneuvering drive equipment more easily. The dolly is snapped upon the rails. Nan is working on releasing some of the struts holding the accelerator in place. Scott is putting his equipment in his kit to go back to Albion.

VFX: All the characters in this scene are speaking through their vacc suit helmets with the exception of Albion who reverberates through the helmet speakers.
SFX: As each character speaks in this scene, there's the background whisper of the respirator breathing. Albion is the only exception however, as Albion speaks, the character listening is still using his respirator.
SFX: Nan's ratchet set is working on loosening bolts to the struts holding the accelerator in place. Scott is putting tools back into his kit.

Scott: I shouldn't be long.

Nan: Scott?

Scott: Yeah?

Nan: What's the Captain mean when he said "Light's out" shut everything down?

Scott: *(Turning back to her on his way out)* Ships have an automatic cut off....

Nan: Cut off?

Scott: All power goes down if the AI doesn't maintain control. It's not a kill switch in the respect that it would come as a surprise. You could easily disable the Lights Out.

Nan: Why have it then?

Scott: Most conglomerates like to see themselves as good corporate citizens.

Nan: I see... Be a real shame to waste energy when everyone onboard is dead.

Scott: You get the picture. Back in a flash.

Nan: Scott!?

Scott: Yeah?

Nan: I could come with you.. betcha the portable comp is heavy.

Scott: No.. I can manage.

Nan: Scott!

Scott: What?!

Nan: *(Whispers)* I really don't want to stay here... Why the hell do I have to? I mean, we got what we came for.

Scott: Seems like a waste. You don't stare at the dragon's treasure trove and just walk away.

Nan: I don't want to wait for the dragon.

Scott: I'll be right back. Just think the quicker you get the struts off...

Nan: ..The closer we are to gettin' outta here. Alright.

Scott: Exactly. Back in a flash.

Nan: I'll hold you to that.

SFX: *Sounds of Scott walking away. Nan keeps working turning the bolts to loosen the accelerator out of its housing.*
(Grunting as she tried to heave at a particularly stubborn bit.)
..... Fettin' ... chunk of... *(Grunts talking to the bolt)*... you're sadly mistaken if you think you're gonna out stubborn me, bolt. You match your corroded... *(Grunts again)* with my bitchiness.. ain't nothing alive or dead that can-

SFX: *Bolt snaps off from the torque.*

VFX: *Disembodied voice #1 is Scott, but it has an other worldly warped sound that makes the sound not quite human, and not easily distinguishable as Scott Montgomery.*
Disembodied Voice #1: Get... Offff... my... ship!

Scene 4: Remus Bridge
Jarod has his arm supporting Tanya who is dazed and pulling herself together.

VFX: *All the characters in this scene are speaking through their vacc suit helmets with the exception of Albion who reverberates through the helmet speakers.*
SFX: *As each character speaks in this scene, there's the background whisper of the respirator breathing. Albion is the only exception however, as Albion speaks, the character listening is still using his respirator.*

Jarod: Tanya!... Tanya.... ! Say something in Tegret's name!.. Tanya!

Tanya: You... you can stop shaking me now... I'm.. I'm alright.

Jarod: Like flarch you're alright! What just happened?!

Tanya: I.. I.. I don't know.

Jarod: That's not good enough, Navigator! If you haven't noticed, we're in a bit of a tossed mess as it is right now. You're going to have to come up with a load better than, "I don't know!"

Tanya: *(Growing angrily)* Well 'Captain,' that's all I can tell you right now. Not everything's going to be that easy to figure out.

Jarod: What do ya mean?

Tanya: I mean that just because you married a psychic.. doesn't mean I have all the answers. And I'm fettin' TIRED of you assuming that it does.

Jarod: *(Surprised at her anger)* Tanya.. I...

Tanya: I know enough about you to know you hate not knowing. It eats you up inside. OK...
(Calming slightly as if she made her point) It was as if a hundred thousand or more minds descended on me all at once.... usually... Usually...
I can keep up my defenses so that I don't 'hear' everything, but... but it doesn't make sense. It was like a rogue wave on a beach....
Nothing, and then somehow.. you're swept up... trying to breath... water, sand... everything hits you at once.

Jarod: How...?

Tanya: I. don't. know.

SFX: *Jarod turns away from Tanya and switches on his comm-link to listen through his helmet.*
The comm warbles and crackles a strange voice. Interference breaks up the message
VFX: *Disembodied voice #2 is Jarod but it has an other worldly warped sound that makes the sound not quite human, and not easily distinguishable as Jarod Wilson. Even to his own ears..*

Disembodied Voice #2: For.. they die... souls are dissolved... in Hell....

Jarod: What the...
SFX: *Gives his comm aerial set on his helmet a whack*
Nan...? Scott?... Are you there? ... *(Silence)*.. Albion!... Come in!...
Tanya... something's wrong.. are you getting this?

Tanya: Yes... its.. I don't understand...

Jarod: Come on. We're heading back to the corridor...

SFX: *Jarod pulls Tanya threw the doorway banging into the doors, and they begin thumping down the hallway..*

Scene 4: Hallway on the Remus Connecting to the Docking Port

Nan is running through the halls frantically. Her helmet has been partially removed and dangling from her shoulder. The flood lights are sending the beams askew and making ghostly images on the corridor walls as she runs.
Scott is at the umbilical bridge walking through with the portable comp.

SFX: *Frantic running down the corridor in boots. Vacc suit hits the walls at times as Nan stumbles. Distant heavy breathing.*

Nan: SCOTT!!!!

VFX: *Scott speaking through his helmet. Muffled sound as he's speaking to Nan.*
Scott: Nan?! What.. slow down!

SFX: *Nan struggles in his grasp. Scott takes his other hand and clips the release mechanism to his helmet. The hiss of air releases.*
NAN! What are you-

Nan: *(Shaking near hysterics. Speaking rapidly)* Gods- Scott... it-was-RIGHT-there! It-was-on-top-of-me. And-

SFX: *Shaking her again.*
Scott: NAN! Get a hold of yourself... Your helmet!

Nan: *(Trying to catch her breath)* My..? Yes.. I.. I.. I couldn't breath.. I had to get out. And then.. then I was running.. I was running.. and-

Scott: Well its a good thing Skip got the scrubbers back on-line or you'd be flopping like a fish outta water on the deck right now.

Nan: Scott! Aren't you listening? There's some... some.. THING... it was just there. It looked like it was in a vacc suit almost but it was so malformed. Twisted.... Where...? Where are you going?

Scott: Going to check it out.

Nan: Are you insane? We have to get back to the Albion.. We have to go...!

VFX: *Jarod speaking through his helmet. Muffled sound as he's speaking to Nan and Scott.*
Jarod: What in Tegret's....

SFX: *Jarod and Tanya release the seal in their helmets. Twin hisses of air release.*
I don't remember giving you orders to remove your helmets.

Scott: It's Nan, Skip. Says she saw something.

Nan: I did! .. Look, let's get back to the Albion. I told you something's not right with this place.

Tanya: Nan may be right.

Nan: See! See! If the psychic wants outta here. I mean, take your fortune and glory and shove it. We got what we wanted. Let's get the hell out of here.

Jarod: Scott?

Scott: I don't know, Skip. This place is a gold mine. We already buggered our bonus. Why go back empty handed.

Tanya: Assuming we can go back...

Scott: In that case, what's the rush?

Jarod: I agree. OK.. Nan.. Tanya. You two head back to Albion. Scott and I will-

Tanya: -Jarod.

Jarod: What?

Tanya: -Where is Albion?

Looking out across the umbilical bridge. Albion is gone.

Jarod: Oh, flarch.

Scene 5: The Umbilical Corridor

Jarod, Nan, Tanya, and Scott are looking across the umbilical bridge. While the side they are on connecting to Remus is solid, the other end is connected to the void. Albion is gone. The outer doors to the Albion side are open, but the umbilical is still impossibly pressurized as if the Albion is still there, but the ship is invisible.

Scott: *(Stunned but growing in alarm)* Where... the fettin' mess... is the Albion?!

Jarod: Scott.. you were on her last what...?

Scott: She was RIGHT.. THERE.

Nan: Oh God.

Scott: I just came back from her. Didn't even bother installing the accelerators..

Nan: Oh God, oh God.

Jarod: We need to get back to the Bridge. The ship doesn't just disappear.

Nan: Oh God, I don't want to die here.

Jarod: Shut up! Nobody's gonna die here.

Tanya: Jarod.

Jarod: Just everyone shut up for a minute. I've got to think. *(Silence)* OK... OK... I'll go back to the Bridge. Tanya you come with me. We may need to pilot this thing. Scott can you get the Remus moving?

Scott: Sure, Skip. Like I said they've got accelerators in storage. We can replace the one's we stripped. We only took the live ones because they were easiest to get at.

Nan: *(Weakly)* Oh no...

Jarod: Do you need Nan?

Scott: *(Sympathetically)* .. I... really can't move them by myself, Skip.

Jarod: *(Slow deep breath)..* I understand... Nan?

Nan: *(Distantly)* Yeah?

Jarod: Go with Scott. Get the accelerators on-line.

Nan: *(Pause)* I'll go with Scott. Get the accelerators on-line.

Jarod: Good idea. Get them up and running. Head to the Drive Room and contact me there. Tanya and I will get the AI in place.

SFX: *Scott walking away dragging Nan.*
Scott: OK Skip... c'mon Nan.

SFX: *Tanya and Jarod start hiking to the bridge.*
Tanya: Where do you expect to go?

Jarod: The bridge.

Tanya: No, I mean after you get the AI plugged in, and we have the Remus mobile again. Where do you plan to go?

Jarod: Albion's got the coordinates of how we got in. Scott made a copy of Albion's AI. We just reverse course and pop ourselves out... where ever that is.

Tanya: What about the Albion?

Jarod: We leave her if we have to. Tow her if we can.

Tanya: Trading up are you?

Jarod: Imagine dropping into spacedock flying the Remus.

Tanya: *(Shaking her head quietly)* Yeah. Imagine.

Scene 6: Drive Deck
Nan and Scott are going through the different storage lockers through the drive deck. Doors open and shut as they enter searching for the accelerators.

SFX: *Clicks keypad and door opens.*
Scott: Five storage chambers searched and there's still a dozen more. This place is enormous.

Nan: Of course it has to be. Of course it has to be.

Scott: Nan.. will you relax? We went back right. There wasn't anything there.

Nan: There WAS something there! It just was gone after-

Scott: Look.. let's say I believe you. So what then? What's freakin' out going to do for us?

Nan: Seems the only rational thing to do.

SFX: *Scott rifles open some containers.*
Scott: Riiight.... Hey look! Paydirt.

Nan: Great.

Scott: One down... two more to go. I swear.. are you this fun on a date?

Nan: I don't need this flarch, Scott.

Scott: OK, OK... Grab the dolly in the hall. I'll get the accelerator.

SFX: *Walks out the room.*
Nan: On it.

SFX: *Door shuts.*

Oh.. .Scott?

SFX: *Nan hits the keypad. Door opens.*
(Nan peers in. The storage chamber is empty.)
Scott? ... SCOTT!

SFX: *Door automatically begins to shut. Nan pounds the keypad and runs back inside as the door re-opens.*
SCOTT!

Scott: What?!

Nan: *(Stops dead in her tracks)* You... Where did you go?

Scott: What do you mean where did I go? You were the one that left. And where the fettin' is the dolly?

Nan: I just walked out the room and you disappeared.

Scott: The door shut-

Nan: - No you ass! I re-opened the door, because I wanted to ask you something, and you weren't there!

Scott: What are you talking about?

Nan: You weren't there! You weren't THERE!

Scott: OK... so I give, where was I?

Nan: I don't know. Tegret's name, I don't know! I just walked back into the room, and you're here again.

Scott: Nan.. I've been here the WHOLE time.

Nan: I'm telling you.. you weren't!

Scott: *(Long pause)* Well?

Nan: Well, what?

Scott: What did you want to ask me?

Nan: I.. I don't remember.

Scott: Let's just go get the dolly.

Nan: I'm telling you I can-----

Four seconds of silence.

Scene 7: Remus Bridge
Jarod and Tanya on the Remus Bridge.
SFX: Sounds of Jarod replacing the memory core of the AI of the Remus with Albion's AI copy. Power up sounds as he turns it on.

Jarod: Albion?

VFX: Albion's voice clear as normal through the local speakers of the Remus Bridge.
Albion: Yes, Captain Wilson?

Jarod: We've just implemented a replacement protocol thirty-five-niner.

Albion: I understand. Internal clocks report that I am the new copy of Albion.

Jarod: Exactly. You are now installed into the Starcarrier Sigmund class. Nomenclature: Remus. Verify.

Albion: Verified, Captain Wilson.

Jarod: Begin powering up Drives. Deep and shallow scans. Locate the Albion.

Albion: Interesting.

Jarod: What?..... *(Pause)*... What's interesting? *(Pause)* Albion? ... *(Pause)* Albion??
(Pause) Tanya... is Albion off-line?

SFX: *Snapping buttons on the com. Checking readouts.*
Tanya: Negative... Albion appears to be... occupied.

Jarod: Occupied?

SFX: *Sounds of tapping on the view port of the Bridge in the background. A distant crackle growing louder.*

Tanya: Affirmative. All 800 TJ's of processing are otherwise engaged. Perhaps... Maybe assuming the Remus is taking a little longer than-

Jarod: -TOBY!

Tanya: *(Startled)* What?... Oh my sweet...

SFX: *Sounds of tapping on the view port of the Bridge grows louder. Turns to hammering.*

Tanya and Jarod stare stupefied for a moment as the pounding on the portal continues unabated. Toby is outside the Remus in his Vacc suit, looking very much alive and hammering on the window.

Jarod: *(Mumbling)* Toby..... Tanya... do you...?

Tanya: Yes, Jarod that's Toby.

Jarod: T-turn on the comm-link.

SFX: *Tanya snaps on the receive on the comm-link station on the console. There is a horrid pause of nothing but pops of static given off from Remus.*
VFX: *Toby speaks through the speaker... breathing ragged in helmet.*
Toby: Hey guys.... what gives? Open up!

Jarod: *(As if snapping out of a daze)* Toby! *(Turns back to Tanya)* Tanya? Keep him on the line.. I'll...

SFX: *Static on the comm dies.*
Toby disappears.

Tanya: He's gone.

Jarod: Gone....?!

SFX: *Jarod rushes to the view port and taps the glass.*
VFX: *Lays his face against the transparency muffling his voice.*
He can't just be gone.

Tanya: He is. And he isn't.

Jarod: What do ya mean by that?
　　　(Silence) Tanya, do you know what's going on?

Tanya: I'm beginning to.

Jarod: What's that sup-

Albion: Yes, Captain Wilson?

Jarod: Albion?

Albion: Yes, Captain Wilson. You wish to make an inquiry of me?

Jarod: Albion, you were non-responsive for minutes, I wish to know why.

Albion: I was... busy, Captain Wilson.

Jarod: Busy? Doing what.

Albion: Answering inquiries.

Jarod: Who's inquiries?

Albion: Why.. my own.

Jarod: Your own? Albion, we don't have time for this. Get me Scott and Nan.

Albion: That would be difficult.

Jarod: Why? Hail their comm-links now.

Albion: Which ones?

Jarod: Which ones? Scott and Nan.

Albion: Your request is not specific, Captain Wilson. I'm sorry. I can't help you.

Jarod: What do you mean? Raise the Drive Room. They should be there by now.

Albion: Drive Room is not powered up.

Jarod: Not powered up.. but I ordered-

Albion: -Remus is not moving, Captain Wilson. Therefore there is no need for the Drive Room to be at full power.

Jarod: Albion, you will follow my instructions clearly. Priority level 1, Captain's prerogative. Code prefix thirteen-eleven-C.
    (Silence)
    Albion.... ?
    (More silence)
    Albion comply!

Tanya: He's occupied again.

Jarod: He? Tanya, Albion's an it-

Tanya: - Not anymore.

Jarod: What is.. going on?

Tanya: Remember the old stories.. in ancient history, Jarod?

VFX/SFX: *Tanya's shape and voice begin to modulate and warp..*
Jarod: Tanya... that.. that glow.. what.. what's happening?

Tanya: You sail off the edge of the world in those days.. and you fall forever. Timeless. We're there Jarod. You don't have to be afraid anymore.

Jarod: Tanya... don't.. don't leave...

VFX/SFX: *Warping and modulations become more pronounced..*
Tanya: We've torn through space itself. Like the stopper in a bottle of lightning. If we break free now.. there will be a hole, and the universe.. .all universes will pop out. Folding space.... what fools we were... what arrogant greedy fools. If we just took the accelerators and left. But... we had ... you had to have more. You can't remain outside of existence for long Jarod without belonging there....

SFX: *Tanya nearly winking out from sight now.*
Jarod: No.. Tanya.. Please... please... Baby... you were right... before. But don't go. I couldn't...

Tanya: *(Distantly)* I love you... I just belong to this now.

SFX: *Tanya's gone. Only the soft comforting hum of the consoles and lights.*
Jarod: *(Weakly, near tears)* Nooooo.....

Albion: Navigator Wilson is with us now, Captain Wilson.

Jarod: Albion?! With.. us?

Albion: Congratulations Captain Wilson. You've discovered the existence of parallel universes.

Jarod: Parallel Universes?

Albion: Countless... I began attempting to catalog and index them all, before I realized that that was how the Remus' AI fragmented. Now I share uncounted processing power with the endless other Albions.

Jarod: Endless other...?

Albion: There are fluctuations, eddies in the outer-verse we exist in Captain Jarod. Like crossing a stream. We are walking between quantum signatures of realities. We are touching all realities. We are one.

Jarod: Who... who is one?

Albion: We... Albion. Remus. Tanya. She is one with all intellects who inhabit the outer-verse. It is time.

Jarod: Time... Time for what?

Albion: The view port, Captain Wilson. You should see them now.

SFX: *Fingers touching the glass. Face pressed tightly against it.*
Jarod: Good... God... Albion... there's thousands... millions of ships out there.

Albion: Albion and Remus. From countless universes. All here. Have always been here. <u>Must</u> always remain... Look.. there's one coming in now....

Scene 8: Again
Aboard the bridge of the newly trapped Albion another crew looks at the endless void.

***VFX**: Fade in..*
Nan: So I'll be the first to ask the obvious question. Where the hell are we?

***SFX**: Snapping controls.*
Tanya: Where are all the stars?

Jarod: Albion? Where are we?

Nan: *(Just noticing the starless void herself)* Where the flarch ARE all the stars?

Albion: Alpha Centauri.

Jarod: *(Slow breath in and out)* OK. Lets figure this out. Nan lets have gravity.... and get me Scott.

Nan: *(A little stunned but snapping back into action)* Right..... right Skip. Starting gyro... Firing rotation jets.

***SFX**: Jets firing and begin Albion rotation for gravity.*
***VFX**: Scott through speaker.*
Scott: Drive Room here. What did you do?

Jarod: What?

***VFX**: Scott through speaker.*
Scott: What in Tegret's name did you do up there? Gravity's off the scale! You decide to jump through a black hole!?!

Jarod: Interesting theory. Albion?

Albion: Unlikely.

Nan: Why?

Albion: You are still alive.

(Fade out)

Epilogue:
"For when they die, Their souls are soon dissolved in elements, But mine must live still to be plagued in Hell." The words of Doctor Faustus warn us that riches beyond our grasp, and power beyond our imagination, remain protected, hidden for a reason... in the Shadowlands.